THE TALE OF TWO NECKLACES

BY MICHAEL STONE

One World Press
Chino Valley, AZ

DEDICATION

I would like to dedicate this book to my family who supported me and encouraged me to never give up.

To all my friends at YEI (www.yeiworks.com) and especially Art who never grew tired of my questions.

And to a dear friend Anita, who without her help this book could never have been written.

TABLE OF CONTENTS

CHAPTER ONE
JANUARY 1ST - JANUARY 7TH 1990

Sunday, January 1st

At ten P.M. on the other side of our galaxy, on
the planet Farth in the small town of Ed, in the state of
Zonastorm in the Great Circle Land a scientist worked in
his lab. The scientist's name is Pop and he is an owl. Pop's
lab was in the basement of his house. Pop finished his
work and locked the door to the lab, and went upstairs to go
to bed.

Around ten-thirty a white pickup truck pulled up in
front of Pop's house. A fox got out of the truck wearing a
ski mask, all black clothing and was carrying a large black
duffle bag. The fox snuck up to Pop's house and took a
crowbar out of his bag using it to quietly break into the
house. The robber knew about Pop's lab and quickly made
his way there, where he knew there would be valuable

objects to steal. He went to the basement door but found it secured with a combination lock.

"No problem," he said quietly with a smile on his face. He took bolt cutters out of his bag and quickly cut the lock.

When the fox entered the lab he saw four locked metal boxes on a rack, two on the top shelf and two on the bottom shelf. He went to the box on the bottom left shelf and used his lock pick to open it. Inside he saw an envelope full of hundred dollar bills which he put in his black bag. He picked another box and when he opened it he saw a necklace with a red heart pendant hanging on a chain of red beads. As he picked the necklace up a voice inside his head said, "Excellent." He knew this had to be a special object so he carefully put the necklace in his coat pocket. The third box contained two smaller plastic boxes which he put into his black bag to look at later. The last metal box contained a necklace just like the other but instead a blue heart pendant hung from a chain of blue beads. The fox heard no voice this time; he placed the blue heart necklace in his duffle bag and zipped it shut. He took the bag and hurriedly left the house; he threw the bag onto the seat of his truck, got in and drove away as fast as he could.

At ten forty-five Professor Pop woke to the noise of the truck speeding away. He grabbed his glasses, turned on the lights and went to check all the rooms in his house. When he reached the basement he found the door to his laboratory wide open with the cut lock hanging useless from the latch. When he entered his lab he saw all of the metal boxes lying open and empty on the lab floor.

"Oh no!" he cried in panic as he ran to the kitchen to call the police.

Meanwhile the robber was driving as fast as possible and in a couple of hours was halfway across the state. He was thinking about how much money he was going to make selling the stolen goods he had, when again he heard a voice in his head say, "Sucker." Then, he saw a glowing red light coming from his coat pocket and yelled, "What the heck is going on, what is in my pocket!"

He tried to pull the necklace from his pocket but lost control of the truck. He hit the curb and two tires blew out. He tried to gain control of the truck but it was no use. He screamed in horror as his truck slammed into a huge oak tree. The fox was thrown from the truck and landed unconscious on the ground.

Next to the tree was a sign that read, "Welcome to Sunsky City."

Red Heart Necklace slid out of the crook's pocket and onto the grass. She looked around and saw the welcome sign. This would be a good place to hatch her plan. "Thanks for getting me out if that stupid metal box and for the ride sucker!" she said as slithered away.

A few minutes later Blue Heart Necklace worked herself out of the black bag through a tear in the side. She slid out of the truck door and onto the grass. She also saw the sign and realized evil Red Heart was loose in the town. She would have to follow Red Heart to protect the city until Professor Pop could help her.

As Blue Heart moved away from the accident scene a car pulled up next to the truck. A badger got out and walked over to the fox that lay injured on the ground, "So why were you driving like a crazy animal?" The badger looked on the ground and saw two boxes lying next to the unconscious animal. "These must be pretty important for you to risk your life to have." Important enough for the badger to take the boxes hoping there might be something inside he could sell for a tidy sum at his pawn shop in the Cruddy Fair Neighborhood.

Monday, January 2nd

The next morning at six, in a blue two story house an alarm clock went off and Shara got out of bed. She struggled up from bed because she was quite heavy. Shara was an eighteen year old white bunny. She had short curly blonde hair, blue eyes, and a red nose. She was five feet tall and weighed two hundred pounds.

Shara's mother knocked on her bedroom door and told her it was time to get ready for school and to eat breakfast. Shara got dressed for school and went down stairs to eat.

At the breakfast table Shara's mother told her, "Shara, I know you are starting a new school today, I'm sorry but the other schools are all full, this was the only school that had an opening."

Shara said sadly, "I don't believe I have to go to this school. I have heard only horror stories about P.T. Coe High."

"I know this will be tough but you only have half of your senior year left. I will also ask the Katholic priest, Miracle Bill the dove, to give you a blessing for these hard times."

Shara said, "I might not like this school mom, but I will go and finish this year as positively as possible."

Shara's mother said, "I know you will. Be careful and pray to the great Dolphin God for guidance and protection."

After breakfast, her mom gave Shara a kiss and a hug and told her again to be safe as she left the house to catch the bus. On the bus other young animal kids were looking at her oddly and making rude comments about her as she tried to find a seat.

The bus driver yelled, "Stop picking on the new kid, if you keep it up I will report you to the principal!"

The bus arrived at school at eight; the students filed off and made their way to their lockers. Shara made her way to the hallway where the paper from the office said her locker was located. As she was walking along she noticed again that everyone stared and made rude, mean comments about her looks. Shara was hurt and afraid that she would not find any friends at her new school. Her locker was a top level locker, number 777. She loved the number seven. Maybe today would be her lucky day.

As she opened the locker to put her backpack and other belongings away Shara heard a gentle voice say, "Hey cool, a new locker buddy."

Shara turned around to see who was talking and was surprised to see, by the lower locker, a leopard dressed as a punk rocker.

The punk rocker introduced herself, "Hi my name is See Nosey," she said as she offered her paw to shake with Shara.

Shara saw that See Nosey has orange fur with black spots. The leopard had bright blue eyes and her short hair was dyed a shocking pink. See Nosey was tall and thin, she wore a black leather jacket with silver studs, black T-shirt, black pants and bright red high top sneakers. Shara decided right off that she liked See Nosey.

Then, the girls heard a boy's voice next to them chime in and say, "How are you doing? I'm Larry Wonder and I am a brilliant scientist."

"He's modest and shy too," See Nosey joked and Larry laughed.

Larry was the same age as See Nosey, seventeen, they had been friends for years. Larry was an otter. He was taller than both girls and he had brown eyes and fur. His hair was jet black and neatly combed. He wore khaki pants and a long sleeve white shirt with a front pocket. In the pocket was a pocket protector full of pens and pencils. He wore immaculately clean white sneakers.

Shara introduced herself and for the next few minutes the three new friends talked and got to know each other a little better. Suddenly, someone in the hall said, "Lookout, here comes the Negative Gang!"

See Nosey said, "Oh no, not them again."

Shara asked, "Who are they?"

See and Larry began to explain to Shara about the Negative Gang. They told her the leader of the gang was a greedy no good bully lion named Claw E. Shred. James Opposite, a tiger, was Claw's second in command and he did whatever Claw told him to. Pat Negative, also a tiger, always liked to be negative so he was a perfect fit for the gang. Hooky Clincher, a weasel, was famous for cheating and stealing and Andrew Confused, a hyena, had been the last member to join the gang. Andrew was silly and liked to laugh a lot. He was much nicer than the rest of the gang and it seemed he really didn't belong in the gang at all.

Shara and her new buddies quickly walked to the cafeteria to avoid the bullies and to continue talking. They talked until they heard the bell ring for classes to begin.

Shara's first class at eight-thirty was English, as she entered the room she pulled down her red shirt nervously. The class stood to say the Pledge of Allegiance. Shara and the rest of the class stood, faced the nation's flag and began reciting the pledge she had been saying for years. "I pledge allegiance to the United Circle Land and to the flag for which it stands, one nation under God, indivisible with liberty and justice for all." Math was next at nine thirty, Science followed at ten thirty. Lunch was at eleven thirty where Shara sat with See and Larry.

"I wish we had at least one class together this morning," said Shara to her new friends.

"Yeah, us too," both See and Larry said together.

As they started to eat their lunch Shara noticed that See was busy combing her short shocking pink hair. Shara hadn't noticed that Andrew Confused was sitting at the table behind them until she heard him whispering to See.

"So why is Andrew whispering to See?" Shara asked Larry quietly.

Larry whispered back, "Don't tell anyone, but See and Andrew have a crush on each other."

"Oh," replied Shara. "Then why does he hang out with that horrible gang?"

"Because, he thinks being mean is entertaining, fun and cool. He believes all the TV shows he watches where being mean is sometimes funny."

Shara and Larry watched as Andrew slyly passed See a note and whispered, "Wednesday night, don't forget our date." Then he stood up and said quietly, "Well, I have to get back to Claw or he'll pound me for sure." and he flattened his yellow spotted ears.

See was excited about her date with Andrew and her orange fur fluffed up. Shara laughed and asked her where they were going on their date.

"See sighed happily and said romantically, "Somewhere in my large bathroom like on the TV show 'Saved by the School Bell'." But quickly she changed her attitude back to her punk rocker persona, "But only if I don't mind."

See and Shara wanted to go outside for some air after lunch. In front of the cafeteria See said, "I need to come with you, never go outside alone because it can be dangerous."

Shara asked, "Why?" as they walked out the door.

Suddenly they heard a big rhino shout to an ox, "Hey you dumb ox, you wanna get beat up? Come on over here and make my day!"

The animals charged one another and started fighting, and their two friends joined in. Luckily, the vice

principal saw the fight from his office window and called
the police who showed up in three cars with six officers
in each car. The officers stopped the fight and carried the
bullies off in handcuffs.

See turned to Shara and said, "See, trust me you
don't want to go outside alone around here."

Shara nodded and swallowed with big eyes and
said, "I won't."

The next class was P.E. where they were playing
basketball outside. See helped Shara, because Shara was
very clumsy and missed the ball a lot. After P.E. was study
hall from one until two and then Music from two to three.
See loved music and so did Shara. Music was the last class
of the day and Shara was very anxious to go home and get
away from the dangerous school, but she knew she would
have to come back tomorrow. She was glad she had found
new friends to help her be safe and careful.

The bell rang and the teacher said, "Class
dismissed, have a nice afternoon."

Shara grabbed her pink backpack and headed for
the school bus. She noticed that her shoe was untied so she
bent over to tie it not noticing that her backpack was not
zipped all the way. In the bushes behind her something had
been waiting patiently for the right animal to come along.
Blue Heart Necklace swung out from a branch on the bush
and landed in Shara's backpack. Shara finished tying her
shoe and got on the bus. She sat next to See and the two
girls talked until Shara's bus stop.

As Shara walked into her house her mom said,
"Dinner will be at five when your father gets home." Then
her mom nervously asked Shara about her first day at P.T.
Coe High.

Shara said, "Let me put away my stuff and I'll tell
you all about it." Shara walked upstairs to her bedroom
and threw her backpack on her bed and left it. She didn't

notice something crawling out of her backpack. Blue Heart Necklace made her way under the bed and waited.

Mom and Shara sat down on the couch in the living room and Shara told her mom. "The school is scary but I made some good friends."

Mom said, "Don't worry, I will call Miracle Bill and ask him to pray for the school to get better."

"Thanks Mom," Shara replied with gratitude.

They got ready and had a supper of lettuce and carrot stew. Half an hour after dinner the news came on at six and her parents listened while Shara did her homework.

The news announcer said, "Channel 4 News with Lin Sue Chatty Gorilla and Nicky Nick Monkey with Adam Willy Peacock foreign correspondent and Steve Walden Groundhog with the weather."

Lin Sue Chatty began the evening report, "Today in local news Professor Pop Owl's laboratory was robbed last night. Police found the robber's crashed truck and recovered the stolen money but other stolen items were not found. According to our interview with Professor Pop the missing items are two necklaces and two watches. Police said that Professor Pop was very frighten when he found out these items had not been recovered. However, because these items are considered top secret we are not at liberty to give descriptions of them to the general public."

Nicky Nick continued with the news, "In Morld News, in Big Oval Country another bank was robbed. This makes the sixth robbery this year. The only evidence police found was a symbol of a fist holding a machine gun which had been painted on the bank wall and motorcycle skid marks on the street. The bank vault door had been ripped off its hinges and police think a motorcycle gang was involved.

"My goodness," said Shara's mom, "The news was really bad tonight."

"Yes, it certainly was," agreed Dad.

After the news at seven Shara went to her room to play video games, her favorite was Mimtendo Nario. At eight her mom called up the stairs that it was bedtime, so Shara turned off her game, got in her pajamas and went to bed.

While Shara was sleeping Blue Heart crawled up onto the bed laced herself around Shara's neck and connected the clasp. Shara continued to sleep soundly, not knowing her life was about to change.

Tuesday, January 3rd

At six in the morning Shara's alarm clock buzzed and she sat up in bed and stretched. She felt funny this morning. While she was dressing she noticed she felt lighter, taller and she could see her feet!

Mom called just then, "Shara breakfast."

"I'll be there in a minute," Shara called back down the stairs. She was still puzzled about the changes to her body. She went to the bathroom mirror and stared in shock at long straight blond hair instead of her usual curly short style. Her red nose was a soft pink, and she was very thin and taller, and very pretty. Shara stepped on the scale and it read 130 pounds instead of 200! She was taller than her normal five feet, she might even be taller than her dad. Shara was excited and scared. Something had changed her...but what? The Blue Heart necklace was invisible to Shara, so she had no idea it was there around her now slender neck.

Shara's mom came up the stairs to check on her daughter in the bathroom, when she saw Shara she screamed "AAAAAARGH," and fainted.

Dad heard the scream and came running up the stairs. "Hey girls, what's going on?" he asked. Then he saw Shara and exclaimed, "Oh my goodness gracious, what's going on here?"

Shara cried, "I don't know, I woke up like this!"

Dad said, "You are not going to school until we see the doctor, I'll call for an appointment, you try to wake your mother up."

Shara tapped her mom's cheek and said, "Wake up Mom, it's still me."

Mom woke just as there was a loud knock on the front door. "Oh no!" Mom cried, "It's Miracle Bill, what are we going to tell him?"

"Oh tell him the Dolphin God gave us a miracle, I'm busy trying to call the doctor," Dad said.

Mom went downstairs and let Miracle Bill in and she told him what Dad had said. Miracle Bill, a white dove with yellow hair, looked up the stairs at Shara and said, "Goodness, all Hail the Dolphin God, it is a miracle." Then he fainted too.

Dad shouted from the phone, "Get him up, everyone can't faint!"

Shara dumped a glass of water on the priest's head and he woke up sputtering.

Dad shouted, "Hurry up and dress Shara, we have an appointment with Dr. Badger in fifteen minutes at seven-thirty."

Mom asked, "What do I tell the school?"

Dad yelled, "Tell them she has the measles."

While Mom called the school, Dad asked Miracle Bill if he would stay and try to calm his wife down.

Bill nodded his head yes, then asked, "But who will calm me down?"

Dad and Shara got in the car and drove quickly to the doctor's office.

Doctor Badger came to the door to meet them and hustled them into a private room.

He ran all sorts of tests on Shara and reported, "According to all my tests, she is perfectly normal and healthier than before. I have no idea what caused this change in her appearance. Go ahead and go home and call me if anything changes again," he said.

They checked out with the medical assistant Felisha the cat. Felisha had orange short fur, green eyes and red hair and she was exactly the same size Shara had been yesterday. Felisha said, "Shara, you have certainly changed, you are gorgeous!"

To which Shara's dad said "Yes she is, I just hope she's okay."

As they left the office, Felisha wished she could be as pretty and thin as Shara.

As the office door closed Red Heart crept in along the wall and slid like a snake into Felisha's purse as it lay on the floor by her desk.

Dad and Shara drove home and reassured mom and Miracle Bill that Shara was not sick but that she did need to rest. The priest left to go home and blessed the whole family as he left, muttering under his breath, "They will probably need it!"

Since it was almost noon Mom made vegetable soup for lunch, Shara's favorite. But Shara noticed she wasn't able to finish the whole bowl because she felt full. She had always had to eat a lot before this miraculous change to feel full.

After lunch Shara went upstairs to read, still not knowing about the invisible Blue Heart necklace around her neck. She fell asleep until four that afternoon when Mom called her to help with dinner. The family ate at five and then watched the end of the show Full Pouch with Bob

Legit the kangaroo. At six they watched the news.

"In local news tonight: in Sunsky City there was a jewelry store robbery, but nothing was taken because the robbers were found tied up by the police. The surveillance cameras showed the robbers and then a person dressed as a blue knight burst through the front door to catch the intruders. Despite the guns pointed at him, the knight had a sword ready to slash down and turn the bullets back on the robbers. You can see the robbers duck for cover and then charge the knight with their fists. He fought them all, knocked them unconscious and tied them up for the police, but the super hero left before any officers arrived." the announcer finished.

"I'm here with Chief of police, Chief Ramstein the ram, "What do you say about this blue knight?" asked the reporter.

The Chief replied, "We have the crooks and they are being taken to jail. People need to let the police take care of dangerous criminals like these and not try to be a hero, you could get hurt. But we thank whoever helped, and he seems like a great crime fighter.

"Next on Morld news," the TV announcer continued, "In Big Oval country another bank was robbed and of twenty security guards hired for extra protection, eighteen were killed and two survived. The survivors reported that only one gunman had killed all the other guards, even though they used every shot they had nothing seemed to touch the robber and he did not appear to be wearing a bullet proof vest or to be injured at all.

"This guy could not be stopped, he was un-animal!" one survivor told police

The reporter continued, "The robber was described as a rabbit, about seven feet tall, weighing two-hundred and fifty pounds, with extremely large muscles in his legs and arms. He has long braided brown hair with a bandanna tied around his head and all black fur. He was dressed in black pants, shirt, and boots and riding a motorcycle. One survivor placed his age in the early twenties. If you see this animal, do not approach, he is considered armed and dangerous. Call the your local authorities," The reporter continued, "Also in Morld news there was another bank robbery up north in Triangle Land. This robbery was done by a gang wearing purple clothes, ball hats and masks, and the leader was dressed all in red. The bank teller reported there were nine animals and they got away with $5,000,000.00 triangle dollars. The Mounties are offering a reward for any information that leads to the arrest of the robbers. Remember, this gang is considered to be armed and dangerous."

Dad said, "I understand robbery gangs, but not one man killing a whole security force and not being hurt by bullets, that has to be an exaggeration."

Little did he know he would soon eat his words.

Since it was already seven, Shara's mom suggested Shara go to bed early to be ready for school the next day.

"If you feel any pain at school, let us know," mom said.

Shara brushed her shiny white teeth, took a shower and curled up in bed to sleep.

About ten-thirty across town Felisha was just coming home from her errands after work. "Whoa, what a day" she said aloud as she placed her purse on the table beside her bed. It started with Shara's beautiful, but strange change. Why couldn't something wonderful like that happen to her? After a quick shower Felisha tuned off the lights and crawled tiredly into her bed. Quietly the purse on the table shook and the zipper opened, Red Heart Necklace wormed out of the pocket and onto the bed and around Felisha's neck as she slept.

Wednesday, January 4th

Five-thirty in the morning Shara awoke to a voice in her head saying, "Shara get up and go downstairs and watch the Channel 4 News." Shara swung her feet over the edge of her bed, but instead of floor, Shara felt her feet touch something else. She looked down and there was a five foot long blue glowing metal staff on the floor.

"Take the staff and do not be afraid," said the voice.

Shara did as the voice told her. She picked up the staff and went down stairs and turned the on the TV. She saw a story about ten animals trapped on top of a burning apartment house. Blue Necklace then took over Shara's body, changing her clothes into a blue top and pants and gave her a blue crown. Shara found herself running down the street very fast, about one hundred twenty miles per hour!

Animals in cars turned their heads and wondered what had just zipped past them, some in amazement, and some in shock. Shara stopped instantly on the backside of the burning building, tapped her blue staff on the ground three times and then rose up on the blue circle that formed under her feet. She flew smoothly to the top of the building and waved over one of the trapped animals and pulled him onto the circle, held him gently and floated down to the ground safely.

He said, "Who are you? I'm seventy years old and I've never seen anyone like you."

"I am the Blue Princess," Shara heard herself say as she rose up again for the next animal. Then, Shara saw a figure in blue armor racing toward the roof moving even faster than she had. She got to the top of the building as the

blue figure rescued two more small animals, one under each
arm. Shara smile as she pulled a large ox onto her circle
and started down again. In only a few minutes the two
heroes rescued everyone off the roof.

The firemen were struggling to put the fire out.
They did their best but still it spread.

The Blue Knight smiled at Shara and suggested,
"Let's put this fire out, shall we?"

"Sure," she replied.

He ran left and she ran right, opposite ends of the
building. Shara again tapped her staff once and water
exploded from the end pointed at the fire with three times
the force of the fire hoses. The Blue Knight raised his
sword and an even bigger water spout came out of the tip.
The two streams met in the middle and drowned the fire
completely.

The firemen, bystanders and TV crews jumped
back and cheered saying:

"Where did all that water come from?"

"Hooray!"

"Who are those two blue super heroes?"

As the water drained into the storm sewers in the
street, the Blue Princess and the Blue Knight went towards
the firemen standing in front of the building and asked if
everyone was alright.

The TV crews stared for a moment and then news
reporters ran up behind the two super heroes and stuck
microphones in their faces shouting:

"Who are you?"

"Where did you come from?"

"Why did you help?"

"What are your names?"

The Blue Knight held up a hand and the crowd
grew quiet. "I'm the Blue Knight," the young man said.

"And I am the Blue Princess," said Shara. "And we
are here to help all animals in trouble."

"We live in this city and we love it," the Blue Knight continued. He lifted his visor and Shara realized he was a handsome wolf with beautiful brown eyes, black hair and silver-gray fur. He was tall and very strong.

At seven in the morning Shara's dad flipped on his usual early morning TV before work. He shouted, "Honey, look Shara's on TV!"

"Oh my, it is her, my baby!" mom screeched as her hands flew to either side of her face "And what is she wearing?" mom said as she swayed.

Dad grabbed her shoulder to steady her and said, "Oh no, don't you faint on me again."

Meanwhile, Miracle Bill was watching TV in his kitchen and said "The Dolphin God has done another miracle for Shara." and then he fainted... again.

Bill's housekeeper, a brown dove with black feathers on her head, threw a glass of water on the priest to wake him. She was used to his fainting.

Shara's mom and dad raced downtown in the car to get to Shara. Shara waved when she saw them drive up and tapped her metal staff three times to change her clothes back to normal, the crown and staff disappear, and suddenly she was back in control of her body. The Blue Knight had just left so she hopped into her parent's car.

Both Mom and Dad yelled together, "What happened, why did you leave the house, what were you doing?"

"I don't know," Shara answered, "It was like I wasn't in total control of my actions. I could still think for myself and I wanted to help, it was well... like someone was helping me. And I had some sort of magical powers with the blue metal staff I found by my bed. When I saw the news report on TV I just had to save the animals in danger."

"Young lady, you are staying home from school again today," Dad said sternly.

Mom asked, "Should we call Miracle Bill for another blessing?"

Dad snorted, "All he did last time was faint."

"Okay, call the doctor then," Mom said. "We have got to find someone to explain all this."

They got back to the house around eight and Dad called his office to let them know he wouldn't be in.

His boss asked, "Is it because your daughter was on the news?"

Dad said, "Yes, yes that was my daughter. As he hung up the phone he said, "Let's go to Dr. Badger, Shara."

Back at Felisha's house her alarm clock went off late and she ran to the bathroom to get ready for work. When she glanced in the full length mirror she screamed in surprise and shock, "AAAAAAHHHH what's happened to me?" Then after a second she said, "OHHH, I am beautiful!"

Her fur was shinier, her red hair was now down to the middle of her back, and her claws were longer, sharper and harder and painted bright red. She was thinner and taller with white, pointed razor sharp teeth and her green eyes were sparkling. Felisha felt stronger and faster as she jumped across the room. Her closet was somehow full of thin clothes and she grinned as she dressed. She ran to her statue of the Cat Goddess Paravati and lit some incense in thanks for the answer to her prayers. Little did she know that she was now under total control of Red Heart Necklace.

Felisha thought, "What should I do about being late for work?"

Then she heard a voice in her head saying, "Call and say you are sick, you are too beautiful to waste time at work."

"Yes," she thought. "I am better than all the other animals now, and besides, think of all the guys I can flirt with today." Felisha called her office and easily lied, and then went out to have fun all day.

Dad and Shara returned home at ten that morning and Dad told Mom, "The doctor still doesn't know anything, but they were expecting us because they had seen Shara on the news with the Blue Knight.

Mom said with a frown, "Well, the Channel 4 news animals were here after you left wanting more information for the repeat broadcast tonight, but I told them to go away, our life is none of their business."

Shara asked, "Mom, Dad, I am tired, do you mind if I rest?"

"Sure, you definitely need it dear," said Mom.

Dad sighed, "What a day...again." He went over to open the window shade to let in the sun. He jumped and yelled, "Honey, what are all the neighbors doing watching us? They have binoculars and are on our patio and sidewalk."

"Yes, I know," mom answered. "I had to shut all the curtains after the news animals came to keep everyone from looking in."

Dad rolled his head in disgust and closed the curtains. "I hope they get tired and go away soon," he said.

****

At the mall Felisha found a space and parked her car. With an air of arrogance, Felisha walked into the mall believing that she was beyond doubt the most beautiful animal in the Morld.

She went into a fancy, expensive clothing shop in the mall and looked around until she saw a full- length, red, sequined dress on a mannequin.

"You," she ordered the clerk, "Get me that dress," she said and pointed rudely.

"Okay," said the girl in a shaking voice

The dress fit perfectly and Felisha chose to wear it

immediately.

"Keep the change," she said as she dropped her money on the counter.

As Felisha left the store several male animals turned to goggle and whistle at her. She just smiled and laughed at their attention. Felisha shopped all afternoon buying new clothes, shoes and jewelry. By the end of the day she had spent all of the money in her checking account, about four thousand dollars.

At four Felisha went home exhausted and happy. This had been the best day of her life ever!

****

At the same time, Shara was just waking up from her long nap and came down stairs to help with dinner.

After dinner Dad said, "Mom, Shara, we need to watch the news to see Shara in action." They agreed and sat down in the living room as Dad turned on the TV.

The TV announcer said, "Channel 4 News, in local news tonight we'd like to tell you about two superhero animals that saved ten animals from a burning building this morning. Here is the video replay."

As the family watched, Mom and Dad's jaws dropped and Shara exclaimed, "Did I do all that???"

"Oh baby, you were in danger," Mom cried.

Dad reassured Mom, "Obviously, something is giving Shara superhero powers and protecting her."

The TV announcer continued, "We have no idea who the Blue Knight is, but the Blue Princess has been identified as Shara Sallie."

"Oh darn," Dad cried. "Now everyone will be here watching us!"

Mom asked, "Do you think the President is watching?

At the White House, President Bald Eagle was

watching the news and ordered, "Have the FBI check out these two young animals, this might be a hoax. If they are real superhero animals I want to hire them to help the country reduce our rising crime rate."

Back at Shara's house, the news continued, "And now for Morld News: in Big Oval country a 20 yr. old female animal was choked to death by the same mystery man who has been robbing banks. According to her crying, sad family, she was dating the rabbit and he called himself Angry Machine Gun Muscle. He had a tattoo on his arm in the same design of a fist and gun as was left on the bank robbery walls, and he matched the description of the other eye witnesses perfectly. This latest death brings the total to nineteen animals he has killed. We now have a picture of him from his driver's license; please notify the police or Big Oval military if you see him. Please remember this animal is a killer and is dangerous."

Dad frowned, "Not this ridiculous story again about the bulletproof crime animal, oh brother!"

At the end of the news the phone rang. Mom answered and said it was for Shara.

It was See Nosy wanting to know all about Sahara's adventure that morning. Shara told her everything that had happened and asked See Nosey to call Shara's other friends, so Shara wouldn't have to tell the story ten times over. See Nosey agreed and hung up. Immediately the phone rang again and it was Larry Wonder, the otter scientist kid from school. He asked Shara for details about her powers that she just couldn't answer.

Larry asked, "Was this a publicity stunt for a movie?"

"Of course not!" Shara said as she rolled her eyes, "I just don't know what is going on with me!" and she hung up. She needed some time to process what had happened to her.

At eight PM Shara told her Mom, "I can't answer

any more phone calls, I'm going to bed."

As she started to brush her teeth, Shara caught a blue sparkle from around her neck and Blue Heart Necklace finally appeared to her. "Are you the power that changed me and made me a superhero?" she asked softly in amazement.

"Yes and I will continue to help you save animals in need and defeat evildoers." The voice in her head replied.

"Why me?" Shara asked.

"Because I saw your good heart and brave spirit,." Blue Necklace said.

Shara crawled into bed and whispered, "Thank you"

The necklace responded, "Sleep well and sweet dreams."

Across the county, Professor Pop packed to leave for Shara's town after having seen the superhero news story. He thought he knew where at least one of his lost necklaces was and the other would not be far away.

Thursday, January 5th

Shara got off the school bus at eight AM glad to be back at school. Mom and Dad had finally agreed she could go back today and she looked forward to seeing her friends. Shara was immediately surrounded by See Nosey, Larry Wonder and other interested students, who chattered and talked at her. Another bus pulled up and to Shara's surprise, a tall silver wolf got off. He was dressed in a black shirt, pants, and had a 50's slicked back hairstyle. He caught her eyes and smiled at her and she smiled back. She felt like she already knew him. Shara and her friends had to hurry to make their first class and Shara noticed she ran easily and kept up with the others. She had never been able to run before. Blue Necklace was helping her again.

At lunch, see Nosey and Larry Wonder sat on either side of Shara to protect her from so much attention from others.

Shara asked See Nosey, "How was your home bathroom date?"

See Nosey answered, "We ate vegetables and tofu sandwiches on a blanket in the big empty tub."

Shara smiled. See Nosey was really nice but kind of weird. Then she continued politely, "Anything else?"

"Yeah," See Nosey bragged. "We had a boom box and listened to the new CD by Michael Jacket. And when the light bulb burned out, Andrew fixed if for me and I kissed him. He's my hero" she sighed.

"So where are you two going tomorrow?" Shara asked, hoping it wasn't another too strange bathroom date.

"We're going to a punk rock concert and dance in the aisles." See Nosey said as she smiled.

After they ate, they headed outside. Shara realized she did not feel frightened like she had that first day. In fact, she had confidence in herself.

Suddenly, from two dark alleys across from the school, gangs of tough looking animals, one group with a large "A" and the other with a large "B" on their shirts, erupted into the street and charged each other shooting pistols and machine guns at each other as they hid behind cars and buildings for cover. All the kids screamed and ran inside the high school and neighbors ran inside their houses.

The Principal announced, "Teachers and students, take cover, stay away from windows and stay inside the building until the police arrive."

Shara, See Nosey and Larry dashed for a door then ducked when they heard the guns going off in their direction.

Shara asked as they ran again, "What's this all about?"

See Nosey replied as she caught her breath, "It's the A gang and B gangs. They've fought each other in this area for twenty years now and neither side can win control of this street."

"Why haven't the police stopped it?" Shara asked.

"Well, the gangs scatter all over the neighborhood and hide before the police can get them, and they keep getting new members for those that do get killed or arrested," Larry explained as he puffed trying to catch his breath.

Shara felt a tingle start in her feet and stopped running as she entered the hall. She looked up to see the silver wolf had also stopped in the hall. Shara watched as the wolf looked at his feet and started to change up his body into the armor of the Blue Knight. Shara's tingling spread up her body too and she found herself dressed as the Blue Princess and not in full control of her body again.

Together they ran to the front door and the Blue Knight smiled again and said as he lowered his visor, "I'll take the B gang, if you'll take the A gang."

"Agreed," Shara said with a smile.

They ran in opposite directions to get behind the different gangs. Shara took her blue staff and knocked ten A gang members unconscious before they even noticed her, while the Blue Knight did the same to B gang members using the flat of his sword. But the two were soon seen by the rest of the gang members, who had stopped shooting at each other for a minute to look in shock at the two teens dressed in blue.

The gang leaders shouted at Shara and the wolf, "This is our fight, stay out of it you blue clowns."

"Not when you're risking innocent animal lives," the Blue Knight shouted back.

"Take 'em out!" the two gang leaders ordered their gang members.

Shara glared at the leaders and yelled "Bring it on!" as she tapped her staff three times on the ground.

Shara even shocked herself. She had never been this brave or self-assured before. Her behavior had become totally unlike her normally shy, quiet self, and she kinda liked it.

Then Shara saw the Blue Knight tap his sword on the ground as well.

A hail of bullets flew through the air towards them, but hit the magical shields that had formed around the teens, and fell to the street. When the gang members saw this, some got scared and threw down their guns, turned and ran toward the police cars that were just pulling up, and screamed, "I surrender!!!"

But the worst and meanest animals were still attacking the Blue Knight and Blue Princess with knives, bats and chains. The weapons bounced harmlessly off the shields. The gang members looked down at their bent knives, shattered bats, and broken chains and more of them ran to surrender.

The leaders and henchmen of both gangs ran into the dark alleyways cursing "We'll be back to get you Blue Knight and Blue Princess." Then the gangs disappeared around the corner.

The police arrested many gang members and left, after thanking the Blue Knight and Blue Princess.

Shara felt her body change back and asked the Blue Knight, "What's your real name?"

As he returned to his normal clothes, the Blue Knight replied, "I'm James Hawkins, and you're Shara Sallie right?"

Then the principal announced, "It's all clear now to return to class."

Shara and James went into the same classroom and

sat down next to each other while the other students and teacher smiled at them.

Later that same afternoon at work, Felisha was checking the blood pressures of the elderly animals from the nursing home. Her last patient was Mr. Sunny Seed, the goat who had been her gardener when she was growing up. He was seventy-two years old but looked much older and very sad.

"I was sorry to hear of the death of your wife," Felisha said.

"Yes, it was a total shock when she drowned in Lake Howl. She was the summer camp nurse," he whispered, "I wish I was with her now."

Felisha was unaware that she was holding two red beads from the Red Necklace. She found herself putting them in Mr. Sunny's coat pocket along with a piece of blank paper.

"I hope you feel better soon," she said as she roughly pulled the blood pressure cuff tight.

"Awe," Mr. Sunny yelled, "That is too tight!!"

"Sorry," Felisha said.

Stupid old goat, stop complaining is what Shara wanted to say.

At five that evening, Felisha left the office and went home. She was very tired.

Shara was also getting home at five just as her dad walked in from work.

"Where were you?" Mom asked, "And how was your first day back at school?"

"Sorry I'm late. School was fine, but the news animals caught James and me after school to ask about how we captured so many of the "A" and "B" gang members during the shootout today," Shara said.

"WHAT?" shouted her parents together, Mom adding, "And by the way who is James?"

Shara waved her hands to calm them down and explained, "James Hawkins is a cute silver wolf, he is the Blue Knight that helped me and he goes to my school. He and I magically turn into the Blue Knight and the Blue Princess, I guess, whenever innocent animal lives are in danger. We can't help it. Those two gangs were shooting up the Cruddy Fair neighborhood around the school."

"A wolf, is he a nice Katholic wolf?" mom asked with raised eyebrows.

"Well, he's nice but he told me he is Norman, not Katholic. What does his religion matter?" Shara replied. Mom stilled looked nervous.

"Forget the Blue Knight; are you on TV again Shara?" Dad asked.

"Yes, I think the interview was going to be on tonight at six," she answered.

"Well hurry up girls, let's eat so we don't miss it!" Dad insisted.

Right on time, the Channel 4 News started. "Tonight in local news, the Blue Knight and Blue Princess fought for justice again today, taking on the A and B gangs at the same time during a shootout in front of P.T. Coe High School. Police arrested most of the members after the Blue Knight and the Blue Princess disarmed them with their superpowers. But the ringleaders and their henchmen managed to escape after yelling threats at the two young heroes.

The police Commissioner stated, "These two special animals saved the day again, but regular animals should remember to call the police, and not risk being hurt. Maybe the Mayor should hire the Blue Princess and Blue Knight to use their powers to help us fight crime," he continued. "And now our exclusive after school interview with these amazing young animals," the TV reporter finished.

Mom and Dad listened closely to the interview, and Mom kept patting Shara's hand.

"In Morld news another bank robbery in Triangle land by the same Red-Purple gang who got away with $1,000,000.00. Two security guards were wounded and all the bank animal employees were tied up. The Mounties have no leads except that the gang was well armed with machine guns and pistols and are still at large.

Dad turned off the TV and said, "Finally, regular bad guys and not magical super criminals like in Big Oval Country."

A loud knock at the front door made everyone jump. Mom opened the door to find two large Golden Retriever dogs, dressed in gray and blue suits and ties. "Excuse me Ma'am," one said, "I am Agent Jones, and this is my partner, Agent Harold. We are from the FBI and we would like to talk to you and your husband and daughter about the events of the last few days."

Mom stuttered, "C-C— Come in, can I get you something to eat or drink?"

"No thank you," they answered, as they went into the living room.

Shara moved over next to her dad on the couch to make room for the agents to sit and because she felt nervous. The two agents asked her about all the things that had happened to her and she told them everything.

Finally, Agent Harold asked, "Do you have any proof of this wild story?"

Shara heard the voice in her head again, "It is alright to tap the staff three times."

The blue metal staff appeared in her right hand; she did what the voice said and became the Blue Princess - crown, clothing and shield.

Both Agents jumped to their feet in amazement. "You are real!" one exclaimed. "The President has authorized us to offer you a job with the government as a crime fighter. Talk with your parents and call this number within the next three days with your decision."

He gave her a paper with her job duties and pay as a superhero for the United Circle Country. The agents left after shaking paws with the family.

Shara stared at her parents in shock.

Dad said, "First your appearance changed, you saved animals in danger, stopped gangs, and now the FBI and the President want to hire you. What's next? Taking on the magical robber from Big Oval Country?"

"Dad, I don't know, but I will help animals whenever I am needed."

Dad said quietly, "Anyway, let's all go to bed and we'll figure this out tomorrow. We're too tired tonight."

And so they did.

Friday, January 6th

Shara got up, ate breakfast and her mom said, "We'd like you to stay home this morning so I can talk with you about last night."

"Okay," Shara replied.

Together the family read over the contract and it seemed fair and honest. Dad was worried about Shara being able to finish school. Mom was worried about her being away from home. Shara was worried about her superpowers. They finally finished discussing everything around eleven-thirty in the morning and all agreed that Shara would accept the contract with a change, to allow her to attend regular school when she was not actively working.

Shara called the FBI number and they agreed to the change and told her to go to the airport Sunday evening to fly out for training in Texlass for a week. Shara hung up feeling a little scared but also a little excited. "I hope you know what you are doing," she whispered as she touched the Blue Necklace.

"I do, it will all be fine," Blue Necklace assured her.

Shara's mom noticed her worried face and suggested, "Shara, why don't you check with your friend James to see if he will be going with you?"

"That's a great idea," Shara sighed with relief. She looked up his number and dialed nervously.

An older lady answered, "Who is this?"

"I am a friend of James', please may I speak with him?" said Shara.

"James, sweetie, there is a girl on the phone for you." Shara heard the older woman say.

Then she heard a thumping sound of feet running down a stairway and James answered. "Hello, this is James."

Shara replied, "Hi, this is Shara."

"Hello," James said warmly. "Have you been contacted by the FBI too?" he asked.

"Yes, I'm leaving Sunday for Texlass, will you be there too?" she asked hopefully.

"For sure," he said. "I'll see you at the airport and our families can meet each other. I'm really looking forward to spending time with you Shara."

"I am looking forward to spending time with you too, James," said Shara blushing, glad that he couldn't see her face. "Bye."

"Come on Shara," Dad said happily. "Let's go celebrate your new job with lunch at your favorite restaurant."

"Yeah! Taco Ball," she shouted as she leapt up to go eat.

At the mall, after lunch, Felisha was buying more new jewelry, but the clerk returned her bank card and said, "I'm sorry this card was turned down."

CHAPTER ONE

"WHAT!!!" Felisha screamed as she snatched back the card and slammed her fist on the counter. She turned and stomped out of the store. They have some nerve, denying a beautiful, perfect animal like me what I want! They won't get away with this, she said narrowing her eyes.

The Red Necklace glowed with her anger. Felisha waited until the next customer went into the store and the clerk was distracted. She found herself racing into the store, grabbing the jewelry she wanted, and racing out so fast that all the clerk saw was a blur. Felisha noticed that the clerk, the customer and the mall guard seemed to be frozen stiff.

"I must be moving super-fast," she crowed, "I am too fast to be seen and can take anything I want from this mall!   I wonder what other powers I have."

Felisha next stole a big leather bag and spent the rest of the afternoon filling it with stolen goods until her car was stuffed full. As she was leaving the mall later that evening to her car, she noticed a group of teenage tough looking guys following her. She smiled to herself. They had no idea what they were in for.

"Hey lady, how are you doin' tonight?" called Claw E. Shred, while his gang (except for Andrew Confused who was on his date with See Nosey) surrounded her.

"Better than you will be if you try to cause me problems," she replied.

"Oh yeah, right," Claw E. Shred laughed, "I have a gun and my boys have knives," he pulled a pistol from his black jacket pocket. "And we're a lot stronger and bigger than you, little lady," he continued.

Felisha just laughed a wicked laugh as her clothes changed to fire-red, a red crown appeared and a red metal staff was in her hand. The gang jumped back in surprise and fear, but Claw E. Shred said, "Nice trick, but pretty clothes can't stop a bullet. Stand back boys, I'll handle this."

The gang moved back from their leader clutching their knives uneasily as Felisha moved her fire shield up into a defensive position.

"Try it," she laughed again.

Claw E. Shred pulled the trigger and fired at her repeatedly but the bullets hit her shield and melted down to the ground. Claw E. Shred was scared but couldn't show it or he would lose the respect of his gang. He grabbed a heavy metal baseball bat from one of his gang members and charged at Felisha swinging.

She blocked his swing and her staff melted right though the bat, splitting it in half. Felisha kicked him back and knocked him down with her staff as he shouted, "Get her boys!!"

The gang rushed in together with knives but Felisha spun around and knocked them all down with her staff, melting the knives into pools of hot metal on the ground and leaving the gangsters shaking and yelling in pain with their burned paws, singed fur.

She walked over to Claw E. Shred, put her foot on his chest and held him down despite his struggle to get free. "I'm stronger, faster, more powerful, and obviously, more beautiful than you or your boys." Felisha told him, "But I like your spunk. I'm going to let you and your boys live to be my new henchmen. But you must obey me as your crime goddess or I'll fry all of you to blackened ash!"

Claw E. Shred stammered, "Y-Y yes, ma'am anything you say" as he shook in terror.

"Get up and each of you take one of these beads," she ordered as she pulled several off her necklace. "When it glows meet me here for further instructions. Now scram!" she said.

The gang ran away as fast as they could.

Felisha smiled as she drove home with all her stolen luxuries.

Friday evening at Shara's house, she and her mom

were packing for her training in Texlass.

"I hope you'll be alright," Mom said frowning.

"Oh, she will be fine, "Dad said, "She has superpowers!"

Mom snorted, "Superpowers won't keep her from being lonely for home!"

Dad put an arm around Mom and patted her hand, "I'll miss her too, honey, but it's only for a week. She will be home before we know it," Dad said.

Shara thought, as she watched her parents, "I wonder if James is having as much trouble with his family worrying?"

James, who was across town, was not having as much trouble with his family as Shara. He was having more! Both of his younger brothers and his two younger sisters tore around his room shouting questions.

"Did you really run so fast? How does it feel to be a hero? What is the Blue Princess like? Is she your girlfriend?"

Finally James' Mom and Dad came in and yelled, "Children, James has a long day tomorrow. Leave him alone to pack."

"Yes Mom and Dad," the kids complained as they left.

Mom and Dad immediately started to worry about how James would do alone all week away from home.

Even grandma came into his room tapping her cane, "Oh James, my grandson, a hero just like your Grandpa in Morld War II."

James's dad said, "Mom, James has superpowers, Dad didn't.

"Your grandpa was still a hero in the navy," Grandma said, giving her son a stern look.

"I know Mom and that will never change, Dad will always be a hero."

James wondered if Shara was having the same problems with her family.

Saturday, January 7th

Shara woke up and smiled because she felt so great. She was excited because Mom and Dad had agreed last night to let her have a party today to say goodbye to her friends. Shara had called her friends and they all had agreed to come, even James and his best friend. Shara dressed quickly and ran downstairs for breakfast.

Mom said, "Do you want to shop today for the things you still need for your trip?"

Shara replied happily, "Sure", since she loved to shop with her Mom.

"Do you want to come with us, honey?" Mom asked Dad.

"Heavens no! I've got a football game to watch today; it's Zonastorm State versus Okrahoma Tech for the college trophy!" Dad exclaimed.

"Okay" Mom said and she and Shara left Dad to his big game.

Shara and her Mom spent the morning and yet her mom still had not seen the Blue Necklace, even though Shara had tried on some low necked shirts. Shara could see it in the mirror and sense it even when it was hidden in her fur.

That afternoon at home Shara packed her new clothes in her suitcase and went down to lunch. She said, "I'll set up the party if you'll help me Mom."

"Alright dear, but then you need to rest before your friends arrive," Mom answered.

Later Mom told Shara to get up from her nap.

"Oh no!" Shara cried, "What can I wear, I don't have a party dress! How could we have forgotten to buy a dress for tonight?"

"Relax Shara," Mom laughed, "I bought you a present at the store when you were trying on shirts." She brought out a beautiful pale blue dress with long lace sleeves, and a three tier ruffled skirt.

"It's lovely!" Shara cried.

"Well, you do seem to like blue lately." Mom said smiling.

Shara laughed and hugged her mom. She ran upstairs to dress and get ready for the party. In a few minutes there was a knock at the door.

Dad answered, "Come in young fellow," he said and James nervously walked in to Shara's house. "Nice outfit," Dad boomed as he patted James on the shoulder. James had on blue slacks and a blue pullover shirt. "Shara," Dad shouted up the stairs, your friend is here."
Shara walked downstairs excited and nervous to greet James. "Thank you for coming to my party," she said. She had never seen a more handsome animal. She felt a warm glow come over her when James said with a smile, "My pleasure, you look very nice."

Mom nudged Dad and whispered, "Leave them alone" and then said loudly, "Dad and I will get the food out and then we are going to a movie. Have fun Shara."

As Mom and Dad left, Larry Wonder the otter came in and Shara introduced him to James.

James Said, "I'm glad to meet you. You are the whiz kid in science, I hear."

"Yes, I love all kinds of science and technology and I sort of have a knack for it," Larry replied.

The doorbell rang again and James introduced his best friend, Nicky, a red fox, to the others. The next doorbell Shara answered was See Nosey and Andrew Confused.

"See Nosey, what a pretty silver dress," Shara said.

"Thank you, I got it on sale at the punk rocker

shop," See Nosey answered, "Your dress is gorgeous. I love that blue on you."

Andrew meanwhile was looking at the pile of movies. "Let's eat and watch something," he suggested.

They agreed on Red and Phil's Excellent Adventure for a movie and settled down to watch it and eat all the snacks. James sat by Shara with See Nosey and Andrew sprawled on the floor and Larry and Nicky in chairs. After the movie, Andrew put on his new Michael Jacket album and the girls danced with all the boys until Shara's parents got home.

"What's that horrible racket?" Dad shouted as he walked in the door.

"Sorry," Shara laughed as she turned down the stereo, "We got carried away with the music."

"Well it looks like you had a good time," Mom smiled.

All the friends then said goodbye and left. Shara sighed happily, and after cleaning up, went upstairs to go to bed since her plane left early the next day.

CHAPTER TWO
January 8th - January 14th 1990

Sunday, January 8th

Shara woke up early, excited about her trip. She, Mom and Dad went to church at nine where Miracle Bill's sermon was about Shara and her gifts from David the Dolphin God. Shara turned red and dropped her head in embarrassment, but Dad and Mom sat up extra tall and proud. They went home, finished packing and headed to the airport around eleven for Shara's flight at noon.

"Now don't be nervous, honey," Mom said as they drove, "Flying is a very safe way to travel."

"I know Mom," replied Shara smiling, "I fly all the time."

"Oh my, I forgot!" Mom laughed weakly.

Dad parked the car while they all went in to the terminal to check Shara's bags. On the way to the ticket gate Shara caught sight of James and waved, the two families met and introduced themselves to each other.

"Oh James," said Grandma, "Is this pretty girl the one you talked to on the phone?"

"Yes, Gram", James said as his ears tuned red.

Shara asked James, "Did your minister embarrass you in church today like mine did?"

"Yes, he wouldn't stop asking me to raise my blue sword like the Angel Unicorn Pegasus Noroni on top of our temple" James answered. "Of course, the Angel's sword is a sword of righteousness and mine is just blue," James laughed.

"Ooh, that's worse than I got," Shara laughed.

The families continued to visit and the kid's moms agreed to keep in touch with each other to discuss what the kids told them on the phone.

Finally the plane arrived and Shara turned to her parents and said, "Goodbye Mom and Dad".

"Take care of yourself, Shara," Mom sniffled.

"We'll see you next week, "Dad said, as he and Mom hugged and kissed Shara good-bye.

James and Shara got on the small plane and found they were the only passengers.

"Is this plane just for us?" James asked the flight attendant.

"Yes, please make yourselves comfortable. We'll have lunch once we are in the air. This is a three hour flight but because of the time zone change it will be four P.M. when we land in Texlass," the pretty flight attendant said.

Lunch was bigger and had more food than either Shara or James was used to. First were cheese and crackers with soda pop, then potato soup, salad with juice, and a tofu roast with gravy, vegetables and milk. And a big piece of chocolate cake for desert and after-dinner mints.   "This must be how movie stars eat on planes," James said quietly to Shara.

"I don't know, but I like it!" Shara whispered back. She decided now might be a good time to ask James something she had been wondering since the first time she saw him. "James, how did you get your powers?"

"Well, it happened the day after my birthday. My grandma gave me this really cool blue watch as a present. I didn't want to accept it at first because I thought it looked really expensive and I told her she shouldn't spend so much money on a gift for me. She told me that she had gotten the watch for a good price at a pawn shop next to where she gets her hair done. I put the watch on and, well ... I felt kinda funny but didn't think much about it until the next morning when a voice woke me up and told me to go to a certain jewelry store. When I got up and looked in the mirror I saw I was dressed as a blue knight and had a sword. I knew what I had to do, and well, the rest was on the news that night."

"I remember, my parents and I watched the whole story."

"How did it happen to you?" asked James.

"I don't know how I came to be wearing the necklace. It was just around my neck one morning. I heard a voice too, telling me to go turn on the news. I felt different so I got up and looked in mirror, my whole appearance had changed. But you look the same with or without the watch on." Shara wondered how James would feel about her if he knew what she really looked like.

"It seems to me, in a way, that the watch and the necklace chose us for some reason."

"I think you are right James," Shara said as the stewardess brought them their lunch.

After lunch they talked more and then rested until the plane landed in Youston on the Texlass coast. As they got off the plane a young antelope in a military uniform met them and got their bags. He told them it would be another two hour drive to the base where the FBI people were and where they would be staying. They arrived at six that evening hungry and tired. Shara and James were given a delicious dinner and shown to their rooms where they both collapsed into bed after a very exciting day.

Monday, January 9th

The alarm went off at six A.M. and Shara said while yawning, "Well the first day of training starts early." She showered and dressed then went down the hall where she met James also on his way to breakfast in the mess hall.

As they ate, a white horse in a white lab coat approached and introduced himself.

"I'm Bob the FBI engineer in charge of your equipment."

"What equipment," asked James?

"Just wait and see," Bob chuckled. "But I'm glad to meet both of you. See you later."

The next animal to join them was a tall, red fox. "I'm Major Tom, and I'll be your guide and assistant while you are on base," he said.

"Nice to meet you, we could use a guide, we almost got lost coming to breakfast," Shara laughed.

"Well, I am here to make sure you don't get lost again," he said laughing with them.

Major Tom went over their schedule for the day.

First at eight was a visit to Dr. Beaver to make sure they were in good physical condition. James was embarrassed when he fainted after a blood test.

Shara said, "Don't worry, my dad said lots of men faint at the sight of needles."

The Blue Necklace and the Blue Watch somehow remained unseen by the other animals at the Dr.'s office.

Next, they went to the gym where first they ran as normal animals and then they transformed and ran as the Blue Princess and the Blue Knight. This time they were so fast they looked like blue lightning bolts and the speedometer broke trying to measure their speed.

"Oooops!" said James, "Sorry."

"No problem," replied Major Tom. "At least we know you both can run faster than 150 miles per hour because that's when the speedometer broke."

At nine Shara was asked to show her blue oval flying. She rose up into the sky several miles before they signaled her to come down. Her oval flew as fast as a plane and her shield protected her from wind gusts or turbulence as she flew.

The most fun was at ten when Shara and James got to use their staff and sword water cannons. They practiced target shooting but missed and hit Major Tom and the technicians who all laughed and shook off the water.

"I guess we are not as accurate as we thought." Shara said frowning.

"That's why you are here, to practice. Everyone needs practice to coordinate weapons and tactics. Don't worry, you'll get better." said Major Tom.

"I hope so; otherwise you all better bring lots of dry clothing." James joked.

At eleven they tested the strength of Shara's staff and the cutting strength of James's sword. Her staff withstood all the attempts to break or bend and his sword cut through every test item they presented. Even James was surprised when his sword cut through a solid stone as if it were soft butter.

Lunch was really good; cheese sandwiches, salad, chips and a hot fudge sundae for dessert.

"Wow, I was really hungry," said James as he

finished his third sandwich and reached for the chips.

Shara mumbled, "Me too," through her salad and second sandwich.

Major Tom smiled, "You kids worked really hard this morning and built up an appetite."

"Also, I noticed I was really hungry after each time I used my powers. I think we use up a lot of energy when we transform." said James.

"Does this mean I can eat all the ice cream I want and not gain weight?" Shara asked hopefully.

"Let's see what the Dr. says tomorrow after you get weighed," said Major Tom.

Shara looked at the afternoon schedule and asked, "What time is this, 1300 hours?

The Major explained, "We use military time on base, with a 24 hour day starting at one A.M. or 0100 hours, then 0200 hours and so on until noon which is 1200 hours. So, one P.M. would be 1300 hours. The important thing to remember is that lights out at 20 hundred hours or eight P.M. and we rise and shine at 0600 hours or six A.M. as you would call it."

"I just call it too early!" laughed James.

That afternoon Shara got a chance to show off her flying oval's lifting power by raising different objects. The workers spread a large net and filled it with more and more weight, but the oval easily lifted whatever they added. There seemed to be no limit to the weight Shara could carry with her oval even though it never got larger than a kitchen table. The net gave way before they reached a weight limit. The shield surrounding both Shara and James' ovals kept the teens from falling off, even during a sharp dive or quick turns.

At 1400 hours James and Shara learned more about how to work together as a team and how to time their attacks and defenses to use each of their separate strengths to protect and help each other. They made a good duo and

Major Tom complimented them on their teamwork.

"It's almost like I can read Shara's mind and know what she'll do next." James volunteered.

"Yeah, it's like I can read his mind too," Shara spoke up.

"You can?" James cried as a blush crawled up his cheeks.

"Only when we train or work together," Shara smiled.

James let go of a big sigh.

At 1500 hours everyone met to go over the result of the day's tests and the schedule for the next day. After the staff meeting, Bob the engineer took them to his lab to show them the equipment for tomorrow.

"Here we have your new cell phones with earphones so you can contact each other in the air and the police with just a word," Bob said.

"Oh, can I call my friend See Nosey on it?" Shara asked.

"No, no," Bob said smiling. "It's for crime fighting and emergencies only," he added more seriously.

'What's this amazing silver metal suit?" James asked as he went over to the wall where it hung.

"I call it the Gray Protector Suit. I made it with all the latest scientific gadgets to fight crime. But since we found you two it may never be used." Bob replied sadly.

"Wow, wouldn't Larry Wonder love to get his otter paws on this beauty." Shara exclaimed.

"Hmmm, maybe you two superheroes could use a sidekick. Perhaps my suit will get used after all!" Bob spoke excitedly. "Excuse me, I have to speak to my boss immediately, see you tomorrow," Bob galloped from the room.

Dinner was just as wonderful as the previous meals and afterwards both Shara and James went back to their rooms to call home. Both assured their families that they were fine, not lonely, not lost, and having a great, exciting time. Shara was so tired she fell asleep right after she hung up and long before lights out.

Tuesday, January 10th

Angry Machine Gun Muscle groaned as he stretched and got up from the hotel bed. He was sore and still tired from the last three days which he had spent crotched, hiding on the ship that brought him from Square land to Triangle land. Before that, he had ridden his motorcycle through the mountains of Big Oval Land and Diamond Land for two days to avoid the police and the military at the border crossings. The most difficult time had been the channel crossing from Diamond to Square land. He'd had to buy a ticket on the ferry, but luckily he had plenty of untraceable cash from his robberies. The Big Oval police probably didn't even know he was gone from the country yet.   Angry Machine Gun Muscle was glad he'd gotten by Triangle Land port security so easily but he really wanted to go as soon as possible to United Circle Land where the banks were much richer. He had heard on Morld News about the Purple Gang robbers in Triangle Land and he planned to take over the gang and use them for his bigger robberies in United Circle.   Angry ordered room service for breakfast cleaned up and dressed in his new black leather biker jacket and clothes and braided his long, dark hair for riding. "Now all I need is a motorcycle," he said. He took a cab to the local Darley-Havidson store and bought a new bike. "This is much better than my old one," he told the salesman as he paid for the expensive motorcycle in cash.

Since it was noon, he stopped to eat and then rode to the poorer part of town. He spent all afternoon stopping at different seedy, rundown bars and pool halls to have drinks and ask about how to hire the Purple Gang. At the last bar later in the evening, Angry caught a TV news flash in the middle of the football game. "We interrupt the game," they said, "for a special news bulletin. The United Circle police have reported another mall has been robbed and cleaned out in Zonastorm by an unknown criminal. Jewelry, clothing, and precious stones just disappeared with the only clue being a red streak or flash caught by the security cameras. Clerks reported items were stolen right out of their paws and they saw only a red blur."

"Hmmmm," thought Angry Machine Gun Muscle, "Some animal besides me has some kind of powers. I'll need to visit Zonastorm after I get my new gang. I can't have any competition."

Back in Zonastorm, Felisha was tired after a long day. She changed into her stolen silk and feather negligee and lay down on the bed and sighed. She had enjoyed stripping two more malls earlier that day but was running out of places to put all her stolen goods, her home was just too small. She was going to need to expand herself, malls were too easy. Perhaps banks might be just the ticket. She would give the gang the smaller pieces of jewelry to fence to pay them to keep out of trouble until she needed them for a bank job. With that plan in her head she smiled and fell asleep.

Wednesday, January 11th

While Shara and James kept on training in Texlass, Felisha woke up late in the morning. She got up and dressed and put on her stolen jewelry and gazed at herself in the full-length mirror she had taken from a dress store. She smiled at her reflection. She was absolutely beautiful. Surely there was no animal more dazzling than she was.

Suddenly, Felisha got a strange feeling inside her head and peered closely at the necklace under her chin. She carefully fingered the beautiful necklace holding the red heart in her paw. Could this be what had changed her? She felt sure that it was, and that meant that Shara had to have a necklace too. Only, Shara's must be blue. That would account for Shara turning into the Blue Princess. Felisha needed to think about this new development and how it could help her get what she wanted...power and riches.

A soothing voice in her head whispered, "That's right Felisha, together we can get everything and more."

"Yes," she murmured blankly, staring at herself, "everything and more."

With this, the red necklace finally took complete control of Felisha's mind and body.
"I'm free. I'm out of that stupid necklace and I have a new body to control," she shouted using Felisha's voice. "And I hate the name Felisha," she yelled, "I'm going to call myself Fire Goddess." As she spoke, she called up her powers and her appearance altered. She now wore a blood red crown, a blazing red pantsuit and red high heels, and around her, her fire staff shimmered with a faint crimson flame. "Now, I'm really magnificent and powerful as I was always meant to be," she crowed triumphantly as she admired herself in the mirror.   Enough admiring herself, it was time to get down to business. She returned to her normal clothing and set out to find her gang she had given red beads to.

Across town, Claw E. Shred was hanging out with his gang in the park, and roared as he felt an electric shock and heat from his pocket where the red jewelry lay. All the other animals also jumped and Andrew Confused asked, "What's the matter guys?"

"Nothing, shut up," growled Claw, "Why don't you go to the store and get us all some sodas."

"Sure thing, Claw," Andrew responded eagerly, "I'll be back in a jiffy."

Claw E. Shred mumbled, "We've got to get rid of Andrew, he's too wimpy."   The gang then drove to the mall where Felisha/Fire had told them to meet her.

Fire was there waiting for them. "Hello boys, just call me Fire," she greeted them, "I've got a little job for you. We're going to rob a bank."

"Ah, ah, ah, ah, a bank?" Claw stammered.

"Just relax, all you have to do is get some ski masks and carry the loot to the car and drive behind me as I fly," she continued.

"F, f, f, f, f, fly?" Claw stuttered again.

Fire laughed, "Just follow me." She led them downtown to the Metropolitan Bank, the largest in the city, and parked in front, in the 'No Parking Zone'.

Inside the bank it was business as usual, until the doors swung open and Fire let go a blast of heat and light from the end of her staff. "Down on your faces, nobody moves," she shouted, as all the animals dived for the floor. "Where is the vault?" Fire asked a teller she had grabbed by the throat. He pointed a shaking paw to the left wall. Fire walked over, pointed her staff and melted the steel door from its hinges.

While Fire was distracted, another bank teller hit the silent alarm and all the animals watched helplessly as animals in black with ski masks emptied the vault of money.

As Claw E. Shred and his gang were putting the last bag in the car, they heard police sirens. "Fire, help us, police are coming," they yelled.

Fire pointed her staff at three police cars racing

towards them and blasted each engine. As the police piled out of the flaming cars, they started to run and shoot at the criminals. Fire laughed and raised her flaming shield which dissolved the bullets and drops of metal plopped to the ground.

"Okay, boys, drive," she cried, as she leapt up on her flaming bat wing which shot fire from the back edge and flew away. The police and animals on the street stood amazed in horror as they watched Fire and her gang escape.

Back in Triangle Land that evening, Angry set out to find and destroy Red Dark Dealer- the head of the Red-Purple gang. His informants had told Angry the gang was hiding in an abandoned warehouse.

Angry drove up on his noisy motorcycle and yelled, "Where is everybody?" As he entered the door he felt eyes and guns following his every move.

From the dark corner came a challenge, "Who are you and what do you want?"

I'm Angry Machine Gun Muscle, I rob banks and I have a job for you. I think we can make lots of money together!" he called back.

"We make enough money already," came a voice from the darkness.

"Well, this place certainly doesn't look like you're making any money," Angry jeered, "Why don't you come out and talk to me?"

"Put down your weapons first," the voice in the dark said.

Angry laughed, "I don't have any weapons." The lights came on and a brown coyote in a red shirt and pants came forward keeping his pistol pointed at Angry

"So, you're the leader of the Red-Purple gang?" Angry asked.

"That's me," the coyote replied.

"I'm really here to take your gang," Angry Machine

Gun Muscle stated, "If you give it to me, I won't kill you."

Red Dark Dealer yelped angrily, "What, you take my gang just like that? Think again rabbit."

Angry Machine Gun Muscle turned to the gang and said, "Relax boys, my problem is with Red here, I'm going to make you richer than he ever could. So let us settle this without you." The gang sensed something dangerous about this animal and retreated to the back walls of the warehouse.

"You think you can take me? Come on and try it!" Red Dark Dealer growled as he smiled and pointed his pistol at Angry.

"Shoot if you dare!" Angry yelled then laughed.

Red Dark Dealer shot and emptied his pistol at point blank range right at Angry but all the bullets bounced off him.

Red Dark Dealer cursed and threw the gun at Angry who caught it and crushed it in his fist.

Red screamed at his gang, "Come on you cowards, we can destroy this creep."

But the animals simply stepped further back, one of them muttering "I think we'll just watch this fight, Red."

Red jumped on Angry and stabbed him in the chest with a big knife, but Red's mouth dropped open in horror and the knife bent and bounced of Angry's chest. Red backed up into a corner and grabbed a shoulder rocket launcher from the weapons stash. "This will teach you to try to steal my gang," he said through gritted teeth and he loaded and fired the rocket. There was an explosion of smoke and flame but when the room cleared, Angry Machine Gun Muscle was unhurt and smiling.

Red Dark Dealer screamed, "What kind of monster are you?" and swung the rocket launcher at Angry's head. As the weapon hit Angry it broke into two pieces. Angry grabbed Red by the throat and pulled him down behind some high boxes.

The gang waited, hearing fighting and choking sounds briefly and then silence. Angry came out from behind the boxes and said, "I'm in charge now, any questions?"

None of the gang made a sound. Angry gave them instructions about where to meet him the next day and they left the warehouse silently.

Angry relaxed on the sofa in his hotel room. It had been a good night's work and now he could begin working on what he really wanted.... power and riches. He sat back to watch the news.

"In Morld news," the announcer said, "An unidentified female cat robbed the Metropolitan Bank in Sun-sky-city in Zonastorm, United Circle Land today. She melted the vault door and the engines of 3 police cars with some kind of fire staff before escaping by flying away above the car with her gang following her in cars. She and her gang stole an undisclosed amount of money. Police shooting at the criminal cat reported their bullets hit a shield of heat, melted and fell to the street without doing any damage. This cat is considered armed and dangerous and her powers are unknown."

So, there was another animal with powers like his. He would need to go to Zonastorm to check out this sassy cat. Angry did not like rivals.

Thursday, January 12th

Shara and James woke up to another day of training but they were excited to see Larry Wonder, their otter friend today. Bob the engineer had agreed to let Larry try his metal suit as backup for the two young crime fighters. Larry would be here by ten in the morning Major Tom had said. As Larry came into the room, Shara and James welcomed their friend with hugs and smiles.

"Wait 'till you see what Engineer Bob has for you!" they chorused together.

"I don't even know why I'm here," Larry said in confusion. "But I am glad to see both of you."

"We will explain as we walk to the lab," Shara reassured him. "Come on!"

She finished her explanation as they entered the lab and Larry's mouth dropped open in amazement as he caught sight of the Gray Protector suit gleaming in the morning light.

"This is a multi-functional, independent monitoring, mobile, directional locator, and communications suit!" Larry whispered in awe.

Bob, the horse, beamed and spoke proudly, "Yes, you know your military equipment. But this one as some special modifications I put in myself! Let me show you how it works."

"Okay, you two scientists have fun and we will see you after lunch for training to see how it works," Shara and James called as they left the lab for their own jobs.

Angry Machine Gun Muscle had spent his morning buying respectable clothes and plane tickets for his new gang. They flew to Sun-Sky-City in Zonastorm with no difficulty using the false papers he had bought in Triangle Land. The only trouble he had was keeping his boys from flirting too much with the flight attendants and drawing attention to themselves. The animals checked into a hotel and Angry sent the gang out to buy weapons and ammunition. He still needed to rest a little after his battle with Red Dark Dealer the night before. His powers were immense but they only lasted for a short while and then he had to rest and he didn't want any gang members getting any ideas about taking him when he was tired.

As he slept, Angry dreamed the same dream of his childhood, being ripped away from his mother's arms on his third birthday, a dark man in uniform saying, "This is for your country, boy." He dreamed of the daily painful shots that knotted up his muscles and made his skin feel like it was on fire, and the endless military training sessions that left him bruised and exhausted. Through all his dreams the dark man kept saying, "It's for your country, boy," over and over and over. Angry remembered when he found the file that told about how his mother was murdered the day they took him. He groaned and tossed, dreaming of the fire, blood, and destruction he had brought down on the lab and the dark man, as he screamed, "I'll NEVER work for your country!"

He woke two hours later, sweating and shaking and glad he had sent the gang out. At four they returned with all new gear, happy and excited about their new toys.

Angry said, "I'm going out to get a new motorcycle. I ordered you all room service for dinner so you can look over and get familiar with the weapons. Stay in the hotel.

Angry Machine Gun Muscle took a taxi to the nearest Darley-Havidson store and bought another fancy motorcycle. As he rode away, he heard a voice say, "Turn left." Angry stared around looking for who had spoken but he was alone. He frowned but turned left and rode into the Cruddy Fair Neighborhood, and stopped in front of a pawn shop. Like a man in a daze, Angry went into the shop where a badger worked behind a glass case. Angry saw the black watch in the case and pointed to it. "Give me that watch," he said.

The badger took out the black watch and handed it to Angry saying, "This will cost you two hundred bucks,"

Angry paid the badger and left the shop walking like a zombie. As he strapped the watch to his left wrist he felt a dark presence run up his arm and into his brain. He heard the same voice again, "Angry, I will give you even more power than you already have to wreck your revenge on the animals that tortured you and killed your mother and destroyed your youthful dreams."

"Everyone is to blame and they will all pay for what they did to me," Angry swore as his eyes started to glow deep red inside and the evil Black Watch began to take over Angry Machine Gun completely.

Angry walked out of the pawn shop to his bike and saw a group of seven animals cluster around it wearing T-shirts that said, "AB Blood".

"This is our territory and we want your bike," the leader said as he tapped his bat into his hand.

Angry grabbed the bat away from the leader with his eyes glowing and as he gripped the bat a flame ran down his arm and burned it to ashes. All seven of the animals stepped back in terror and fear.

"You work for me now," Angry growled as he dropped the charred bat to the ground. He gave them directions to his hotel and told them to meet him there later that night and rode off.
The gang members shivered and looked at each other and wondered what they had gotten themselves into. The Blue Princess and the Blue Knight were bad enough to force them to combine their gangs. But this guy was ten times worse. Each one knew, without a doubt, that this animal would kill them if they didn't show up at his hotel.

Friday, January 13th

Angry Machine Gun Muscle woke at noon after a

long night of planning today's bank robbery. They ate and the gang scattered to the pre-arranged locations around the Sun-Sky-City Saving Bank to wait for Angry's signal. At one P.M., Angry entered the bank and shot a burst of machine gun bullets at the ceiling.

At the signal, his new gang rushed into the bank throwing animals down on the floor while Angry shouted, "Stay down if you want to live!"

From the back of the bank, Fire Goddess zoomed in on her red bat glider and yelled at Angry, "What is this? You are NOT robbing the same bank I'm robbing. Oh, it's you."

They stared at each other with a feeling of recognition. The Black Watch's spirit and the Red Necklace's spirit remembered evil times working together before they were imprisoned in the watch and necklace and locked up in the science laboratory.

Angry said, "Welcome Fire," as he kissed her and their eyes glowed red.

"Let's finish this job together, then we can talk," he continued.

"Allow me," Fire laughed as she melted the bank vault door into a puddle of red glowing metal.

Angry and Fire then ordered their henchmen to clean out the money and put it into Angry's van outside the back door.

"Now, don't get lost with all that money because I'll be following you," Fire joked, half serious. She never fully trusted anyone, but especially not the dark Black Spirit.

Sirens started wailing almost immediately after the vault vanished.

"I'll deal with the police," Angry said smiling at Fire. "You can follow that money van to my hideout. Get rid of that young punk gang of yours, we don't want to babysit kids. I have plenty of experienced animals."

Fire turned to her boys and said, "Beat it before

the cops get here, and keep your mouths shut or else. You
don't work for me anymore." She waved her staff and all
the beads flew out of the boys' pockets and back into her
necklace.

Claw E. Shred and his friends raced into the
alleyway and they sped off in his car throwing away their
ski masks and heaving huge sighs of relief.

The police pulled up with two SWAT team vans
with fourteen officers each at both the front and back of
the bank. They ran to the rooftops and windows of nearby
buildings. Police crouched behind ten police cars in front of
the bank and used a megaphone to communicate with the
thieves.

"Throw down your weapons and come out with
your hands on your head," the Police Chief called.

As a helicopter approached, Angry Machine Gun
Muscle came out the front door shooting bullets from his
right hand gun and fire from his left hand. The police and
SWAT teams responded with a storm of bullets which
bounced off Angry or melted in his fire stream. He flamed
the police cars and two exploded forcing the officers and
setting the special team's armored uniforms on fire. As fire
trucks and ambulances roared up to the scene of mayhem
Angry calmly climbed on his motorcycle and raced away.

At the back of the bank, Fire had overcome the
SWAT team and they were now all unconscious and
wounded, unable to stop her escape.

"Get that helicopter back here," one of the team
shouted into his radio as he collapsed.

"Drive!" Fire shrieked to the van driver and he took
off with a squeal of tires. Fire jumped on her glider and
raced up to face the helicopter. "Catch me if you can!" She
howled with glee as she threw a burst of fire at the copter's
blades.

The machine lurched sideways in the air and
dropped, luckily into a park with a pond where the pilot and

officers could scramble to safety to the astonishment of the picnicking animals. Fire whooped triumphantly and flew off to catch up with the money van.

The van, motorcycle, and Fire's glider arrived together at the fancy house Angry had rented earlier that day.

"Park the glider and van in the garage. Unload it and then get into the house and draw the curtains." Angry ordered.

As the gang fell into the furniture and relaxed, Fire and Angry sat down in a sitting room alone to talk. They each told their own story of being captured and escaping the scientists. Fire admired Angry's new body and he told her about its special powers, even before the Black Watch spirit had possessed it. Angry complimented Fire on how well her lovely new body matched her spirit. They talked about future plans through dinner and then settled down to watch themselves on the news.

"Today on Morld News," the announcer began, "In Zonastorm, Sun-Sky-City another impossible bank robbery took place. Last week's unknown fire cat was joined by a mysterious rabbit with bullet proof skin and who shot fire from his left hand, according to eye witnesses. Police reported the injured included: five SWAT team members with serious burns, fourteen with multiple injuries and twelve police officers with burns and bullet wounds. At the hospital there are six animals in critical condition, ten in guarded condition and the rest were treated and released.

"According to Police Chief Ramstein," continued another reporter, "the FBI had joined local law enforcement in tracking these unusual thieves. The mysterious animal mentioned earlier has been possibly identified as Angry Machine Gun Muscle, a rabbit criminal from Big Oval Land where similar crimes occurred. The international police are checking his movements and identity as we speak."

"Oh my!" Shara exclaimed as she and James watched the news in Texlass

"What is going on in our hometown?" James cried.

"I am glad Larry's training with us today went so well," Shara said, "Maybe we can go home tomorrow. It looks like we are needed in Sunsky City.

Saturday, January 14th

As Shara, James and Larry flew home early Saturday from Texlass to Zonastorm, Shara asked James, "So, did your family have a hard time excepting your change?"

Yes, but since the only thing about my appearance that changed was my clothing I think it was a little easier for them because I still looked the same."

"I guess you already know from what all the kids at school have said that I changed a lot. I was not very pretty before the necklace found me. So my family had a little harder time accepting what was happening." Shara looked down as she spoke, she couldn't look at James knowing what he probably thought about how she really looked.

"I saw you around school before the watch and you looked lovely to me then," James whispered, and Shara's ears turned red as she blushed.

Larry was too busy with studying his new metal suit powers to notice the other two. At ten in the morning the plane landed in rainy Sunsky City where the teenagers were met by their happy families. Larry introduced his family to the others and hugs and tears were shared all around.

"Oh, my baby!" Shara's mother cried as she hugged

her daughter.

"Please Mom, not in front of James," Shara whispered as she hugged her mother back.

Shara's Dad clapped her on the shoulder and hugged her booming, "What have they been feeding you, you look wonderful."

"We all worked very hard and they fed us very well," Shara laughed, "but I look just the same Dad. I'm looking forward to a rest," she sighed, "after I call See Nosey, we need to catch up!"

As the families parted, James called out to Shara and Larry, "Remember the radios and use them if you need to."

After Shara and her family got home and ate lunch, her Dad gave Shara the number to call her FBI Bureau Chief, Joe Lock the grizzly bear, to check in. Joe was the leader of the Protector Team of Teenagers and would be assigning them to their jobs and talked about how he would get in touch with her if he needed to. Then Shara called See Nosey and talked about 3 hours on the phone about everything that had happened in the last week, and of course boys. See Nosey told Shara that Andrew Confused had complained to her of being ignored, left out, and pushed around so much by his friends in the gang that he was quitting it on Monday.

"That's great," Shara replied, "Andrew is too nice an animal to be hanging out with those meanies."

At the hideout that afternoon around four, Fire and Angry divided the bank money among their henchmen, and started to plan their next job on Monday. This was going to be a much bigger operation than a simple bank job.

CHAPTER THREE
January 15th – January 21ˢᵗ 1990

Sunday, January 15th

James woke early for Norman Temple services. He asked Larry Wonder to join him and his family but Larry decided not to go to church. He said he was not sure about any religion or philosophy yet but he thanked James for the offer. James told him any time he wanted to attend he was welcome.

During the sermon the pastor and congregation prayed for the injured police and fire animals that were in the hospital.

After church James phoned Shara, "Do you think a visit from the Blue Princess and Blue Knight would cheer up the wounded and their families?"

"Yes, I thought of that in church too," she answered eagerly. "And my dad was going to take me."

"Tell your dad that my father and I will pick you up

at your house in a half an hour," James said.

As the young superheroes walked up to the yellow brick hospital entrance Shara wondered how she would feel in the same situation as these families. She felt herself shimmer into the Blue Princess and saw James change into the Blue Knight.

James reached out to hold her trembling paw and whispered, "It will be alright, I am here for you."

"I just hope I can do something to help them all," she whispered to James.

As Shara watched her fuzzy reflection in the elevator doors Blue Necklace sparkled almost like she was encouraging Shara. Shara and James entered the ward and got permission from the nurses, doctors and the families to visit the police and firefighters.

Inside both their heads the voices of the necklace and watch spoke quietly, "Hold your hands together over the bodies of the injured animals, one on each side of the bed and wish them to be healed."

Shara and James approached a wounded police officer.

"Thank you for all you do to protect animals," said James as he shook the officer's paw.

"Yes, thank you so much. We appreciate you so much," Shara said. Then, she looked into James' eyes and without a word Shara stepped around to the other side of the bed and the two teens held hands over the officer's body and wished him to be healed.

As they stepped away from the officer's bed a nurse came into the room.

"Look!" cried the nurse. "The burns and bullet holes are healing. He will live!"

Shara and James went to each of the wounded animals and healed every one of them.

The families shouted for joy and cried tears of happiness as they crowded around their loved ones.

Shara sagged against James, "I'm so happy we could help, but I'm exhausted."

"Me too, let's go home dad," James said as he gently took Shara's paw in his hand.

In the afternoon in her room at the hideout, Fire Goddess was enjoying her favorite activity - admiring herself in the mirror.

Angry looked at her with disgust and said, "Come away from your stupid mirror. Why are you so vain? We need to plan tomorrow's attack,"

"Of course," Fire said sweetly as she glared viciously at his retreating back.

They joined the rest of the gang downstairs to finish the military base plan.

"We want to rule not only Sunsky City but all of Zonastorm and eventually Great Circle Land," Angry boasted as he spread his arms wide. "For that we need missiles and more fire power to force the leaders of this lousy place to obey us, and we need more recruits. After we make fools of the military and take their missiles no one will be able to challenge us."

"You are such a genius," Fire purred.

That evening as Fire and Angry watched Morld News they heard about the miraculous healing done by the Blue Princess and the Blue Knight at the hospital.

Fire looked seriously at Angry, "We may have a problem here," she said.

"Don't be stupid, we're more powerful than they are. With my new body's extra powers I am unstoppable," he bragged. "Let's get some rest. We will take care of them later."

"Why don't you take the couch, I've got the bed," Fire laugh and flounced off to the bedroom.

Angry walked away from her scowling and said sarcastically, "Whatever you want darling."

Monday, January 16th

Six in the morning on a clear and sunny day, Fire Goddess, Angry Machine Gun Muscle and their gang blasted through the front gate of Duke Air Force Base in Sunsky City. The alarms shrieked and soldiers poured out of the barracks grabbing their M-16 rifles or running for helicopters and jets.

The thieves gunned their ten-ton truck across the runway toward the missile storage building and crashed through the door.

Angry shouted to his men, "Get in there and load those missiles, I'll take care of the ground troops and Fire will cover the air."

He jumped off the truck and turned to face the oncoming military. He shot his machine gun and threw a blast of fire at the animals running toward him, causing them to dive for cover. They shot back but the bullets bounced off Angry. The sergeant gaped and called for heavier guns. Soon jeeps with big machine guns and anti-aircraft guns surrounded Angry. He continued to shoot and throw flames destroying anyone or anything that tried to get past him into the missile building. Even the big guns did nothing to him at all.

Up in the sky, Fire was being chased by a large helicopter which shot heat seeking rockets that exploded harmlessly on her fire shield before they ever reached her. She laughed and shot fire beams blazing back at the copter causing it to crash. As the F-16 fighter planes roared toward her she skipped above them and poured fire on their engines which exploded. The sky filled with parachutes as the pilots and crew struggled to survive. By now, back in the missile building the gang had finished loading six missiles on the truck As they zoomed out of the building Angry jumped onto the front bumper to clear a path out of the compound. When the truck swung around a corner, two of the red-purple gang fell out and were captured by the air force.

"Forget them!" Angry shouted back to the driver. "Keep up your speed."

Fire Goddess sped ahead on her flying bat shield and destroyed the gate that troops were trying to keep closed.

"Disable those tracers on top of the missiles with your narrow laser beam Fire," Angry ordered as they raced away from the base.

In the command center the general shouted, "What were the casualties?"

"49 dead, 75 wounded, 4 F-16's crashed and 2 helicopter gunships destroyed. M-16's, jeeps, and anti-aircraft guns melted and destroyed along with the gate and missile storage building, reported the Lieutenant in a shaking voice.

"What did they get?" growled the general into the radio.

"2 Heat Seekers, 2 Smart Cruise bombs and 2 nuclear warheads." reported the sergeant. "But the two thieves we captured are being interrogated now," he continued.

"Can we track the warheads?"

"Sorry sir, they seem to have destroyed the tracers on the missiles," reported the radar technician.

"We've got birds up looking for them visually but they seem to have disappeared. Get me the FBI on the phone immediately," the General ordered grimly.

At eight that morning Shara walked into the school hallway talking excitedly to her friends, glad to be back in school.

"Look!" See Nosey pointed, "Claw E. Shred and his

gang are in the Principal's office and here come the police."

"Andrew Confused looked scared and said, "I am so glad I quit the gang before school today. Otherwise, I would be in handcuffs like them right now."

All the students stared as the police took the gang away.

"That's what happens when you steal jewelry and clothes from the mall," warned the principal as he walked up to the group of students. "Now everyone go to class."

"Well, I guess we won't have to be afraid of the Negative Gang bullies after lunch anymore," See Nosey spoke loudly. "And if we ever do have trouble with anyone we have the Blue Princess and Blue Knight to help," she finished. All the students agreed and laughed as they went to their classrooms.

FBI supervisor, Joe Lock, phoned the high school and got permission to take Shara, James, and Larry out of class at nine. "National Security," was the only reason he gave.

On their radios he told the trio to go to Duke Air Force Base immediately to look for clues to the robbery of six missiles that morning. Shara and James transformed outside the school and took Larry home to get his suit. The three then flew swiftly to the base.

"What happened here?" cried James as they approached the main gate and saw the twisted metal fence and sentry post.

"That's what we need Larry to find out," said the general who had drove to the gate to meet them. "His specialized equipment in his suit may pick up chemical clues we have missed. Aren't you three a little young for this line of work?" he asked.

"We were chosen and have been gifted with powers far beyond the ordinary," James replied. "I don't think our age matters to the forces that help us," he finished.

Larry scanned the entire base where the fight had

happened while James and Shara went to the base hospital to heal the injured soldiers.

Larry reported to the general and his team what he had found out a few hours later. "According to my instruments, the flame used to melt all the metal is not anything previously known by our scientists. It is composed of organic molecules and comes directly from the staff of the cat and the fingers of the rabbit. However, it is still able to be quenched and put out by water. I found a puddle where the flame hit one side and left scorch marks but there are no marks on the opposite side. The machine gun used by the rabbit are a type found in Big Oval Country and are the same as those used by a criminal mastermind known as Angry Machine Gun Muscle. He also was reported by your men to be untouched by bullets. According to the FBI sources in Big Oval Country, this animal was treated with experimental drugs for years to make his skin bulletproof and to make him into the perfect soldier. Unfortunately something happened in the lab and he went crazy. He killed all the scientists and escaped about a year ago. I think your thief is Angry Machine Gun Muscle," Larry finished.

Angrily, but quietly the general fumed. "What I want to know is can we find the missiles location?"

Larry smiled and said, "I can tell you where the gang was before the theft and that may lead us to their new hideout. I found pea gravel and a rose bush leaf along with fingerprints belonging to a Triangle Land gang that has disappeared and a small local gang that the FBI has been watching."

The lieutenant chimed in, "According to the two animals we captured, the hideout is somewhere in a rich suburb called Moonlight at a rented home. The leader is, as Larry surmised, Angry Machine Gun Muscle and an orange cat who calls herself, Fire Goddess."

"She was identified by a juvenile gang member

Claw E. Shred we arrested for thefts at the mall and the two banks here in Sunsky City," said the chief of police who was sitting across the room. "Also, a nurse, an orange cat named Felisha has been reported missing by her employer. She matches the description of the Fire Goddess perfectly except the Fire Goddess is thinner," he finished.

"Shara and James shared a look remembering Shara's transformation as their inside voices said, "Fire has the red necklace and Angry has the black watch, we can sense it."

The Protector Teens Team flew to the first hideout that afternoon but found no clues.

The FBI supervisor growled, "I guess we'll just have to wait until the criminals make the next move."

Shara, James, and Larry flew home exhausted and disappointed.

Shara's dad joked as she walked in the door of her house, "How was your first mission as a heroine honey?"

"Tiring and frustrating, may I eat dinner now and go to bed?"

"Of course," both her parents chorused.

"I can appreciate now how hard it is to work all day. I can't wait to get back to school," Shara grinned tiredly.

Tuesday, January 17th

On a cloudy, rainy morning Shara and James met at Larry's house for breakfast to plan their search for the missing military warheads. They decided to eliminate places that were too busy or too small to hide missiles, but that still left about a third of the city's industrial area to search.

"The only thing I can do is fly over and look for heat signatures of a large group of people, and then check them out individually, said Larry as he munched on a bagel.

"It will take forever that way," James protested.

"Then we better get started," Shara sighed as she finished her orange juice.

Angry ignored the rain as he walked boldly up the steps of Sunsky City Legislature Building early in the morning. The security guards told him to stop until he opened his coat to show them the dynamite strapped to his chest.

"Get the governor and the mayor down here in the lobby in five minutes or I'll blow this building up!" He roared waving a red switch around in the air. Animals screamed and ran for the exits as police rushed in and surrounded him. Reporters with TV cameras showed up quickly to cover the scene and SWAT team members poured in the front door.

"What do you want?" demanded Governor Soffat, a red-tailed hawk, as he was joined by Mayor Plum, a gray squirrel, at the bottom of the stairs leading to the lobby.

"My name is Angry Machine Gun Muscle and yesterday I stole six war heads from the Duke Air Force Base and I have hidden them all over Sunsky City. They are all connected to this dead man's switch; if you kill me the whole city will be destroyed. I want you to surrender Zonastorm and Sunsky City to me. You have one hour to decide. Call the police and the military, they will confirm what I am saying," Angry spoke as he glowered at the crowd. "Don't try to shoot me, I am bulletproof and if you irritate me I'll blow one of the bombs right now," he continued.

"Hold your places animals, while we check out the madman's story," the Governor ordered.

Ten minutes later a terrified governor and mayor ran

into the lobby, "We surrender," they panted. "What should we do now?"

"First, send all law enforcement and military personnel home under house arrest; if we see them on the street we will kill them. Second, release all prisoners from police stations, county and state prisons and tell them to report to me here. Third, all your state employees in the building must stay at their desks and do as I say. Last, give me the keys to all the important buildings in the city and the governor's offices and then you disappear," Angry said smiling viciously.

He turned to the media "You TV reporters, tell the citizens of the city and state to go home and stay there until I say different!" He stripped off the fake dynamite, laughed and threw it at the police as he headed up the stairs to the old governor's office.

Shara, Larry and James raced to FBI headquarters after having received an urgent call about ten, in which they had been briefed about the events of that morning.

"What can we do?" James asked as the team walked into the FBI agent's office.

"Just keep out of sight, stop any criminals you find and tie them up, and most importantly, find those warheads and defuse them. We know they are scattered throughout the city now and will be even harder to find; but you must find them, until all six are found this crazy animal is in charge," he said. "No military or state troops or law enforcement agencies can do anything right now," he continued.

The Protector Team Teens looked at each other, nodded and said, "We're on it!" as they took off from the rooftop.

By noon the TV news was filled with stories and pictures of animals looting, robbery and stealing, while ordinary animals struggled to protect their businesses, homes, and families with whatever weapons they had available.

Shara said, "Most importantly, we need to protect animals' lives and find the warheads."

"I agree," chorused Larry and James.

James spoke, "I think we need to split up. Larry you look for the warheads using your amplified hearing, vision, and heat sensors."

"Aye, aye captain," Larry joked as he blasted off with his suit rockets.

"I'll radio when I find anything. I'll check on our families and neighborhoods then tap into the 911 system and respond to medical emergencies. I can use my blue oval to carry people to the hospital." Shara said.

James smiled and said, "I think my sword is hungry to punish criminals and stop riots."

Each raced off in a different direction.

Angry sat in the governor's office with his feet propped up on the desk scratching the fine finish. "Get me some food," he shouted to the frightened secretary who ran to obey him.

Fire Goddess sauntered into the office covered with jewelry and shiny clothing and sat on the top of the desk. "Get your stupid baubles out of the way, I'm trying to watch the news," Angry growled. "Isn't it beautiful to see a city destroyed," he gloated as he watched the riots and looting on the TV.

"No, I AM beautiful," Fire snarled, "As if you'd ever notice!"

Angry ignored her and shouted again for his food.

Fire narrowed her eyes and looked at Angry. To her he was just as selfish, stupid, and blind as every other time they had tried to work together. Always destroy, destroy, never having any fun first. She hated him!

As Angry gazed at the TV his mind went to the plans he had made. Fire is useless now. He had the warheads, and the city and state was his. She wanted to waste time gathering shiny junk instead of helping him take over the rest of the country.

Angry sneered, "Fire, make your-self useful and get some food for the animals guarding the missiles."

"Never," she screeched, arching her back and hissing, "Get your city flunkies to do it. I'm too gorgeous and important to be your servant," She stalked out of the office angrily.

As evening colored the sky crimson and gold Shara flew home to rest briefly, glad to see her neighborhood was quiet. Her worried parents hugged and kissed her and took her into the house. The sky grew dark and the city fell into an exhausted sleep.

Wednesday, January 18th

The morning dawned clear, cool, and quiet as Shara flew over Sunsky City. Below her, she still saw fires burning but she also saw firemen putting them out as fast as possible.

"I guess even Angry doesn't want to rule a city of ashes. I bet he told the firemen to go back to work," she muttered to herself as she flew to meet Larry and James.

After the team had gathered, Larry told them he had found two or three suspicious places for them to search. The first place was a warehouse that was empty but had a lot of people going in and out of it. The team swooped in and surprised an illegal electronics ring.

"Too bad we can't tell the police to take these guys in," Larry said.

"What do you mean, son?" said a voice from behind

Larry. "We're here, we are just not in uniform." said a large German Sheppard as he and several other animals came in the door with drawn pistols. "We'll take care of the crooks for you," he smiled. "Even without the police station we have been watching this place for a week. Thanks for catching them red-handed," said the officer.

The second place the team went was an old abandoned factory. Shara peeked in an upper story window. "I see four armed men grouped around a silver canister with a pointed end."

"The warhead!" Larry whispered. "Which animal has the red button detonator?" he asked.

"The one with the red cap on," Shara replied. "He's the one standing next to the pointed end," she finished.

James said, "I'll get that detonator away from him. Shara, you water cannon the other three to distract, and Larry you disable the bomb."

Quietly they climbed in the window and crept to the stairway that overlooked the floor of the building where the bad guys were standing. Shara aimed her staff and waited until James crawled down to the floor below behind the animal holding the red button. James signaled with his paw and as he jumped on the bad guy Shara blasted the other three into the far wall with her water cannon.

One swing of James' sword and the button flew up into the air where Larry caught it. Larry swooped down and pried off the casing and pulled the wires out destroying the arming mechanism. Then he crushed the button detonator. Shara tied up all four animals in the next room and closed the door.

"James, I think I should fly this warhead to the Mythical Mountains east of the city and hide it. Maybe we can lure Angry and Fire out of the city if we can get all the warheads.

James grinned and then laughed, "Great idea, then we can fight them away from innocent animals."

Larry smiled too and said, "I called our un-unformed police friend to come collect the lot."

Shara lifted the warhead carefully onto her oval and flew out of the double front doors. James and Larry flew off to investigate the third location, but it was empty.

Angry waited at City Hall for all six of his animal to call in on the hour to let him know the warheads were safe.

"Where is warhead number four?" he shouted. He grabbed his radio and called Fire. "Group four has not called in, go check it out," he told Fire.

"But Angry, I am having my toenails clipped and polished, I'm too busy," Fire radioed back.

Angry's whiskers flared out and stood on end as he screamed into the radio, "Do it NOW or I'll burn your stupid toenails off!"

"FINE," Fire screeched as she glared at her radio and it melted.

In the city, Fire zoomed over the factory where group four were supposed to be and went in cautiously. She found a radio that had been dropped by the animals guarding the missile and called Angry. "There's no one here, the warhead is gone and so are your men," she reported.

Angry's eyes turned blood red as he spoke quietly to Fire, "Come back to City Hall, we need to talk about our old blue enemies. They seem to be interfering with my plans.

Later that afternoon, Shara, Larry, and James continued their search as well as helping keep the city calm with help from the police, fire and medical personnel, who were out of uniform to avoid Angry's men. The team got together in regular clothes over dinner at the neighborhood Taco Ball, Shara's favorite fast food restaurant.

"Where to tomorrow?" Shara asked as she ate her third bean and cheese burrito.

Larry replied, speaking around his veggie tostada,

"I have three or four places to check out first thing early in the morning."

"Let's meet at dawn at Larry's and get a good night's rest tonight." James mumbled through his fifth cheese taco, "I am exhausted!"

And they headed home.

Thursday January 19th

The day dawned clear and sunny. Everyone met at Larry's house; they were sitting around the kitchen drinking the orange juice that Larry's mom had poured for them.

Larry said, "Like I was saying, there are three or four places I wanted to check out today. There are a few abandoned barns in town where we could look there first. If we don't find anything there, we can check out the junk-yards. After that, we should check out the last few abandoned factories. The last place we could look today would be any empty stores."

Mom said, "I know that you kids are very brave, strong, and have superpowers, but you should be very careful from now on."

"Don't worry Mrs. Wonder," said Shara speaking for herself and James. "Our moms and dads told us the same thing. We will be very careful to avoid Angry Machine Gun Muscle and Fire Goddess."

Larry gave his mom a hug and the team waved goodbye as they ran out the kitchen door.

Because the team moved so fast it took only a few minutes to carefully check several barns. They had no luck, so they moved on to the last barn. It was clear of any missiles too so they marked 'barns' off their list and went on to the junk-yards.

The junk-yards were much harder to look through because they were full of well...junk! After two hours the kids decided to ask the junkyard man for help.

He said, "Sure kids!"

The man used the huge crane to lift and move tons of junk, but no missiles turned up. The team continued on to the last junkyard, hopes still high that they would find more missiles.

As Larry approached the junkyard man at the second junkyard, he thought the man looked suspicious.

Larry called James over and whispered, "Hey, do you think that guy looks shifty?"

James looked at the shady character and agreed with Larry.

The trio talked and decided to go have some lunch and make a plan on how to get into the junkyard. They decided to go to The Pizza Log for some veggie and pineapple pizza.

"I think we should make our move tonight when it is dark," suggested James as the group sat down at a table in the restaurant.

Larry and Shara agreed.

"Okay," said Larry, "How are we going to get into that junkyard?"

"Well, I could fly over the fence and Larry could use his booster rocket to get over. Then, we could check the place out because I am sure there are more bad guys in there," said Shara.

"Yeah, and I bet there is a missile in there too," exclaimed James. "Once you two get in the junkyard and have located any more bad guys you can text me on my cell. I'll be outside watching for anyone coming in."

They all agreed to the plan and decided to carry it out at six that night. As they paid their bill an emergency call came through on their ear pieces.

"EMERGENCY, EMERGENCY! Superhero's, if you can hear me, please come quick. The dam has broken and a huge wall of water is heading toward the city!"

The blue watch whispered to James, "Think big."

"What?" asked James.

"Just think big. Picture yourself sixty feet tall."

"Oh... I get it!" James said and pictured himself sixty feet tall.

First, he changed into the Blue Knight. Then, the harder the thought, the bigger he grew, until he was sixty feet tall!

James looked around until he saw several large boulders. He picked up a few of the biggest ones and stacked them in the path of the oncoming wall of water. The boulders created a second dam and stopped the water from flooding the city.

Back at City Hall Angry had been listening to the radio as the announcement came on about the dam bursting.

"The dam broke? How could that have happened?" thought Angry - then he knew. "Fire Goddess" he said and crushed the radio like a soda can. "She could have ruined all my missiles! I am really going to let her have it when she gets back. I am so mad." he finished with clenched fists.

About that time, Fire walked into the room and Angry did just what he said he would do and started yelling at Fire.

"You big fireball oaf, you could've ruined all my plans, wrecking the dam like that!" yelled Machine as he stormed around the room.

"I did it for you, you big goof! I thought it would wipe out the city a lot faster, and then we could go have some fun." Fire yelled back.

"You could have destroyed all the missiles with that water you moron."

"Well, see if I ever do anything for you again," said Fire as she turned and walk out of the room.

Meanwhile, James went home where his mom had a nice big dinner waiting for him. James knew that he and the rest of the Protectors, Shara and Larry were eating a good dinner too because they had a big job to do that night.

Around six that night the three teens met outside the junkyard.

"Okay," said James. "Does everyone remember the plan?"

"Yeah," said Larry and Shara.

The three teens made a circle, put their hands together in the middle and said, "Let's get the job done!" as they raised their hands in the air.

Larry pushed the buttons on the handles of his booster rocket and flew up over the fence of the junkyard. Shara followed him. They landed in the back lot of the junkyard.

They landed quietly and look carefully around. The junkyard seemed to be deserted it was so quiet. Larry put his night-vision goggles on and looked out across the junkyard.

"We should split up," whispered Shara.

"Okay," said Larry. "I will start in the back, you go to the front and we will meet in the middle. Now remember Shara, try not to let any bad guys see you."

"I will remember. You be careful too," said Shara.

So they searched through the Junkyard without making contact with any bad guys. Shara could move so fast that no bad guys could have seen her even if they had been looking. As for Larry, he had to be more careful since the only way he could be fast was to use his jet pack, and he could not very well do that - it would make too much noise! Larry and Shara met in the middle of the junkyard.

"Did you find any missiles, Shara?" Larry whispered.

In a very quiet voice, Shara told him "Yes I did. They have it hidden in the back of the garbage truck over there. She pointed to the large red garbage truck sitting in the front lot of the junkyard.

"I saw two bad guys walking and looking around the junkyard," said Larry.

"And I saw three bad guys around the garbage truck and one in with the missile." Shara said. "I will take down the two goons walking around while you call James to meet you at the back gate. Then we will all three take on the other four crooks."

"Great idea!" Larry said as he turned to head to the back of the junkyard, taking out his cell phone as he went.

Shara went off in search of her prey. She didn't have to go far when she spotted two bad guys walking along. They looked like Twiddledumb and Twiddledumber thought Shara and she giggled to herself. Shara crept up behind one of the bad guys and fast as lightening Shara knocked him out cold. The other bad guy looked down at the first bad guy and quickly drew his pistol out and shined his flashlight as he turned in a circle.

"Who...who's there?" The bad guy stammered. He knew he couldn't use his radio to call for help because both paws were full, but he said in a shaky voice, "I have a radio and I'm not afraid to use it!"

Shara laughed and the bad guy turned to see where the laughter had come from and WHAM! Shara let him have it. The second bad guy landed with a THUD next to the first bad guy. Shara handcuffed the two with the handcuffs the police had given her. Then she dusted off her hands and said, "Have a nice nap, boys."

Meanwhile, Larry met James at the back gate. Then they ran to meet Shara at the red garbage truck. The team looked from behind an old pick-up at the garbage truck.

James whispered, "You know that Machine Gun Muscle isn't too smart."

Larry asked, "Why do you say that?"

"Because the color red can mean emergency, so a red garbage truck would be the first place to look for a missile."

"You're right! We didn't even think of that," said Larry.

"Okay, how about we each take on one of the bad guys. Then, Shara, you and Larry can go inside the garbage truck and take out the last bad guy. Finally, fly the missile to the mountain.

"Sounds like the perfect plan," smiled Shara.

"On the count of three then," said Larry and he counted - "one, two, three!"

Each member of the team took out a bad guy. Shara and Larry flew up inside the garbage truck and after some yells like "Ouch" and "Help me mommy." from the last of the bad guys, Shara and Larry flew out of the garbage truck carrying the missile between them. They landed on the ground by James.

The two heroes were laughing so hard about the last bad guy calling for his mommy.

"Did you hear him?" asked Larry through fits of laughter.

"I sure did," laughed Shara. "He was really crying for his mommy!"

James looked at his two friends laughing and asked, "What's so funny?"

Shara and Larry told him all about how the bad guy inside the truck kept calling for his mommy.

"That is too funny," laughed James.

"Yeah, for sure." agreed Larry.

On a more serious note Shara asked if all the crooks had been handcuffed.

"They sure have," said the guys.

"Good," said Shara. "Let's get this missile somewhere safe."

Larry and Shara flew off carrying the dangerous missile between them. James radioed the police to come and get the gang members at the junkyard then he took off like a flash. All three headed to the Mythical Mountains.

By nine that evening each super hero was safe and sound at home fast asleep.

Friday, January 20th

The sound of rain hitting against the window woke Shara up. She walked to the window to look out. She had always liked the rain, but today she realized that she didn't just like the rain, she loved it!

"What a beautiful day" she sighed as she changed out of her pajamas and into a pair of jeans and a purple long sleeve shirt.

Shara headed downstairs to have breakfast. When she went to the fridge to get milk she saw a note on the door. It read "Dear Shara, we are going to have to work late tonight because of the current state crisis. While you are home alone don't let anyone in. We don't want to come home to find a bad guy knocked out in the living room.

Shara smiled because she got her parent's joke. As she ate her cereal, Shara thought about her two superhero friends. They had a big day ahead of them. Today they would search the box cars at the train yard. She hoped they would find another missile. After breakfast Shara headed over to James' house.

James' mom answered the door when Shara knocked. "Well, hello Shara. I will tell James you are here. Why don't you go pour yourself a glass of juice."

James came in the kitchen and said, "Hey there Shara, Larry just called and he is on his way."

Grandma Molly came bustling into the kitchen, her eyes opened wide and she grinned. "Well, well James, is this the young lady you told me about?"

"Yes Grandma, this is Shara. Shara, this is my Grandma Molly," James said making the introductions.

"So, Shara, you must be the polite girl I spoke to on the phone." Grandma said as she poured herself a cup of coffee.

"Yes, I am, Grandma Molly, and it is nice to meet you."

About that time there was a knock on the front door.

"That must be Larry," said James as he went to open the door.

"I hope I haven't kept you waiting," said Larry as he walked into the house.

"Not at all buddy, come on in," said James.

Shara said, "Hey Larry," as they walked into the kitchen.

"Okay group, we have a lot to do today. We better get going," James said.

"Right," Shara said, "There are fifty box cars we need to search."

"Well, then let's rock and roll," Larry said.

By noon they hadn't found a thing in any of the box cars they had searched.

"We can't give up," said James.

"No way," agreed Larry and Shara.

In a boxcar not far from where the super heroes stood a dark shadowy figure hid under the boxcar. It was one of Angry's bad guys and he was watching the trio.

Inside the boxcar were six more bad guys guarding one missile. They were listening to music on a boom box.

"Keep it down guys, you know Angry said we couldn't have one of those things in here," said one of the bad guys.

James, Shara, and Larry started walking toward the next boxcar. The bad guy under it started banging on the bottom of the boxcar to warn the others that the good guys were coming.

However, none of the bad guys inside the boxcar heard the banging because the boom box was too loud. As the superheroes got close, the bad guy jumped out from under the boxcar and pointed a gun at the three kids. He pulled the trigger over and over but they just bounced off the heroes' shields.

The six bad guys in the boxcar heard the shots and came running out to attack the kids. Larry, James, and Shara smiled at each other and took on all of the bad guys. In a matter of minutes all seven gang members were tied up and locked in one of the boxcars. James called the police chief at his house.

"Hello," said the police chief.

"Hello chief, this is James and we have seven bad guys locked up in a boxcar. Can you send some men to come and get them?"

"We're on our way!"

Twenty minutes later the police showed up with a big plain white van and hauled the bad guys off to jail. With the bad guys locked up tight, the three superheroes flew the missile to the Mythical Mountains.

"I don't know about you two, but I am starving," said Shara.

"Yeah!" said Larry.

"Let's go get our families and meet at Larry's for dinner to celebrate," said James.

Later that evening around five, the kids and their families were enjoying a great dinner when James' cell phone rang.

"James, this is the director, we have a problem. There is a group of people rioting for food at the Zitty

Super market.

"Okay director, we are on our way" said James.

When the super heroes arrived at the store, animals were marching up to the market with baseball bats and rocks. However, when then they saw the super kids arrive they all stopped. The leader of the riot said "We don't want to hurt you kids, but we need food for our families, so get out of the way".

"Wait!" said James "I have an idea. Just give me a minute to talk to the store manager." James came back out a few minutes later and told the animals that the store workers were going to divide all the food up evenly. This made everyone happy.

"Another disaster avoided," said the super trio, as they flew home.

Saturday, January 21st

James came downstairs to find his two younger brothers and two younger sisters waiting for the first batch of Grandma Molly's delicious pancakes. "Well, it's cold and cloudy out there, a perfect day for pancakes," Grandma said as she took the first batch off of the old gas stove.

"Where are mom and dad?" asked James as he took the first bite of pancakes.

"They are at the diner working," said Grandma.

"Boy, my family works hard at the diner. I think I would rather be a superhero!" said James.

"Oh, it's not that bad," said Grandma. "Your grandpa and I worked there for years and years."

"Grandma, didn't you ever work anywhere else?"

asked James.

"No siree, I worked there 'till I retired!"

"What about Grandpa?"

"No, he worked until he died of a heart attack, the great Dolphin God rest his soul," she said as she touched her heart.

After breakfast, James received a phone Call from Chief Lock. "I want to have an update meeting with the three of you at my house in half an hour. I will call your two friends," the chief said in his deep voice.

"I will be there lickety-split sir," replied James. Then he hung up the phone. "I have to go to the chief's house for a meeting," James told his family.

"You be careful now," Grandma Molly said.

"For sure, love you guys," James said as he waved good-bye to his family.

James met Shara and Larry at Chief Lock's home. They each took a seat in a wooden chair facing Chief Lock's desk. In his deep, gravelly voice, the Chief asked, "So, you kids have found three of the six stolen missiles, is that correct?"

"Yes sir, that is correct," said Shara as she sat in the middle chair between the two boys.

"You have done excellent work so far, but we need the other missiles," the Chief said. "Today you must find the fourth one," he continued.

"Chief, we have a few more places to check out. First, the abandoned houses, then abandoned storage sheds," said James.

"If I had some kind of special visor that would let me see underground, I could fly over places where a missile might be buried, "suggested Larry.

"I can take care of that, said the chief. "I will call Bob the engineer in Youston and tell him to get to work on it right away. He will call you when he has something finished."

"Sounds great!" exclaimed Larry.

"Does anyone need anything else?" asked Chief Locks.

All three kids shook their heads no.

"Alright, this meeting is over. Good luck today."

As the three got up and started to leave a voice came over the chief's radio.

"Chief Lock, this is Police Chief Ramstein, come in please," the familiar voice said.

"This is Chief Lock," the chief said into the radio.

"Sir, we've had a kidnaping, an eight year old female parrot with the name of Polly Ester. She was taken from a park not far from her home."

"Any witnesses?" the chief asked.

"Yes, a neighbor was jogging and said that he saw a dark blue Gord Saurus and that the driver stopped and pulled the girl in through his window." Chief Ramstein said with concern in his voice.

"Do we have a license plate number?"

"No sir, but we have a physical description of the driver from the eyewitness."

"Good, let's have it," said Chief Locks

"Suspect is a male jaguar; approximate age is mid-thirties with black hair and blue eyes." Chief Ramstein told Chief Locks.

"I can spare one of the super heroes to help search for the girl," Chief Locks said.

"Appreciate it sir," replied Chief Ramstein.

"I will send James to meet you at the victim's home. Call him on his cell and give him the address," Chief Locks told Chief Ramstein.

"10-4 sir, and thank you," Said Chief Ramstein.

"James, you go find this little girl," Chief Locks said.

"Okay Chief, I'm on it," replied James as he ran out to go to Polly Esters' house.

"You two better head out and find those missiles. Larry, Bob will call your cell when he has your new visor ready."

"Okay Shara, let's go!" said Larry and they left Chief Locks' office.

When they arrived out on the sidewalk, Larry said to Shara, "We should split up, you take the North side of the city and I'll take the East. If either one of us finds something we will call the other.

"Sound good to me," Shara said as she flew off on her blue oval.

Larry turned on his jet pack and took off for the South side of Sunsky City.

They both thoroughly searched any abandoned or un-rented houses, looking in the attic of any house that had one. Four hours into the search of all the abandoned and un-rented houses, Shara having investigated one un-rented and one abandoned house, entered her second un-rented house and saw there were no missiles, so she headed straight up to the attic.

"Bingo!" said Shara when she saw the missile. She called Larry, "I found a missile and for some reason it is not being guarded right now. Come meet me and we will take it to the Mythical Mountains.

"Great job Shara, I am on my way," said Larry.

Meanwhile, James had spent the last four hours talking with the Ester family and getting pictures of Polly to take with him. The family thanked James and he left as the family gathered around their Buddha shrine to pray.

Next, James found the car the kidnaper had used. It had been stripped clean and on the door an "A" had been spray painted. James knew exactly who was to blame. Then he saw the body of the dead kidnaper sitting in the driver's seat with bullet holes in his back, chest, and stomach. It also appeared he had been hit in the back of the head with a baseball bat.

"What a mess." James said out loud. His heart felt sick with worry for little Polly.

James looked at the skid marks in front of and behind the kidnaper's car. So the A Gang had boxed in the kidnaper to prevent him from getting away. Did they take Polly with them, and if so, why?

James knew the A Gang hung out on this particular street. It was marked with their gang sign showing it was their territory. So, it would make sense that Polly would be in one of the houses on this street. James knew he had to find her quickly because the A Gang's rival, the B Gang, could show up at any minute and then they would fight each other and Polly could be in danger. There were fifteen houses and five three story brownstone walk-up apartment buildings. He decided to search the apartments first. A half-hour later James had searched thee apartment buildings and still no Polly. Then, he heard gun fire and knew the B gang was getting ready to attack the A gang. He had to find Polly and get her out before the fighting started. James swiftly checked the last two apartment buildings then started searching the houses; these would be easier to clear. When James came out of the thirteenth house he saw members of the B gang sneaking into the neighborhood at the other end of the street. The A gang lookouts spotted the intruders and the shooting started. James was thankful that all the gunfire was at the other end of the street.

Before long the street was full of gang members and bullets. James was looking at the fourteenth house when he saw two A gang members looking out the window. He knew Polly had to be in there; otherwise the two gangsters would be on the street fight the B Gang. James ran around to the side of the house.

As he stood listening, he heard an animal burst through the door to the room where the two gangsters stood looking out the window. James heard the animal say, "Hey guys, our gang is getting pulverized. The B gang is not messing around this time. The boss sent me to get the five guys in the living room plus one of you. So, grab your guns and lets go take the B gang down!"

All seven of the gangster ran out of the house leaving one to guard Polly. James knew why the A gang was getting pulverized; the B gang had somehow managed to get guns and flame throwers. The A gang only had pistols and shotguns.

James went around to the back door which he found unlocked. He quietly entered the house. All the gangster saw was a blue streak before he felt something hit him on the head, then everything went black. James found Polly tied to a chair. He used his sword to cut her free. She held tightly to him as he held her with one arm. As James zoomed out of the house he heard victory yells going up. He looked back and saw several buildings on fire and the B Gang holding their guns above their heads as they cheered. There were many bodies lying on the ground, mostly A Gang members. The rest who survived were surrendering to the B Gang. James took Polly home to her very grateful parents.

"Oh thank you," said Mrs. Ester as James handed Polly into her father's waiting wings.

"If we can ever help you in any way just let us know," said Mr. Ester as he held Polly tightly in his wings.

"Just doing my job sir," said James.

When he was outside, he called Chief Ramstein who was very glad to hear Polly was safe and sound. James also told the chief about the gang fight.

"I wish I could send officers over there, but I can't risk letting Angry know they are not locked away in their houses. I can however, send fire and ambulances to put out the fires and help any injured animals. Good job today James," said the chief.

James called Shara on the special cell phones the FBI had given them. They decided to meet at Joker in a

Box for lunch at one.

As they sat down to eat their tofu burgers and fries, Shara and Larry told James about finding the fourth missile in the attic of an un-rented house. James told them about rescuing Polly Ester and how the B Gang had taken over the A Gang's territory.

They were leaving Joker in a Box when Larry's cell phone rang. It was Engineer Bob.

"Hi there Larry, I have your new visor ready. Can you meet me a Duke Air Force Base right away?" asked Bob.

"Sure Bob, we are on our way," said Larry.

When the three super teens arrived at the base they were taken directly to see Bob.

"Well, hello there kids. How are you?" asked Bob.

We're great, Bob," said Larry.

"Give me your helmet Larry and I will attach your new visor."

Larry handed Bob his helmet and Bob talked as he attached the visor. "With this new visor you will be able to see underground and see any missiles that might be buried there. You had a very good idea, Larry."

"Thanks, you did a great job of making it so fast."

By three, Larry was putting on his helmet with the new visor.

"Okay," said Bob, "We need to test the visor. We have buried several objects in the desert around the base. You are going to fly around, use the visor and see if you can find them."

"You got it, Bob," said Larry as he pulled the visor down over his face and took off.

Larry flew over the ground and was amazed that he could actually see objects that had been buried.

By four, Larry had easily found all of the buried objects. "This visor is awesome!" exclaimed Larry.

James said, "Thanks Bob, this new invention is

really going to help."

"You are very welcome, I was glad to help," said Bob with a smile. "You three look very tired," he said with a concerned look on his face.

"We are," said Shara.

Well, we should all head home," said Bob

The kids agreed and said goodbye to Bob as he left to go back to Texlass.

We'll meet tomorrow at Shara's house and make plans to find the last two missiles," said James.

The three super teens flew home. They each took a long hot shower, then enjoyed a delicious meal and shared the events of the day with their parents. Two of them crawled into their comfortable beds and fell into a deep sleep.

 But first, one super hero had a job to do.

As the kids slept, the B Gang leader went to thank Angry for the machine guns and flame throwers.

"Thanks for the fire power. If I can do something for you, just let me know," said the gang leader to Angry.

There is something I want in return," said Angry.

"Name it."

Angry walked over to the gangster and wrapped his paws around the leader's throat.

"I want your gang," Angry said as he choked the life out of the flamingo.

THE TALE OF TWO NECKLACES

CHAPTER FOUR
January 22nd - January 28th 1990

Sunday, January 22nd

After Shara and James got home from their different churches, they went to Larry's house. Larry didn't go to church, but he didn't mind his friends talking about their churches.

Larry's mom had a nice lunch ready for them when they arrived. As they ate they talked about where the last two missiles could be. "Now that I have this cool visor we can look underground," said Larry with excitement.

"Anyone have an idea where they could have buried a missile?" Shara asked.

"Yeah, I do," said James, "I think we should try the graveyards."

"How many graveyards are in Sunsky City?" Shara wondered.

James had already looked that information up last evening

at the public library.

"There are five," said James.

"When did you have time to do the research?" asked Shara.

"While you two were sound asleep I was busy at the library."

He is so brave, handsome, and smart, thought Shara, as she looked at James.

"I drew a map for each of us showing where the cemeteries are. Larry, you start with the Zonastorm State Cemetery. Shara and I will pick up three shovels at C-Mart and meet you there." said James.

"On my way!" said Larry as he engaged his rockets and flew toward the graveyard.

James and Shara got the shovels and met Larry at the Norstorm State Cemetery.

Larry had already covered half of the graveyard by the time Shara and James arrived.

"Do you think Angry would dig up a body and replace it with a missile?" Shara asked the boys.

"We can't put anything past him," said James.

"I have flown over half the cemetery and nothing so far," said Larry.

"Well, keep looking, check out the other half, we can't afford to miss anything," said Larry

Shara sighed, "I wish we could help you Larry, but you are the only one with the ability to see underground."

Larry nodded and said, "That's okay, Shara." Then he flew up to check out the rest of the graveyard.

In half and hour Larry was back and hadn't seen a missile buried anywhere.

"Okay, it's two, let's hit the next graveyard, Sunsky City Cemetery," James said.

"Let's move, Shara said.

Two hours later, Larry announced the cemetery clean - no missiles.

"Wow, that took a long time Larry," Shara commented.

"This is a very big cemetery. The next one, Sleep Slumber Cemetery, isn't as big and shouldn't take as long," James explained as he studied his copy of the map.

"It's a little after four. I can sweep that graveyard in less than an hour," stated Larry.

"Alright team, let's get going," said James.

After only half an hour Larry was back with his team. "I found the missile. Angry had put up a fake headstone to make it look like a real, freshly dug grave. We need to get back there and carefully dig it up."

"We will follow you," Shara told him.

It took the three teen super heroes about half an hour to dig up the missile.

"Let's get this thing to the Mystical Mountains. Shara, you and Larry fly the missile to the mountain. I will stay here and put all the dirt back. When we are finished, we will meet at my house. I'll ask my mom to cook us a really good dinner. She likes doing that sorta thing," said James.

By six that evening, the three super teens were sitting around the table enjoying the delicious meal James's mom had made. "I know Shara, you and Larry stopped by to tell your parents what happened today. I bet they were glad to see that you two were alright," said James' mom.

"Yes, they were," commented Shara.

"I called the commander to tell him we had found the fifth missile," said James.

"What did he say," asked Larry.

"He said there was nothing more we could do tonight, that we should get some sleep and be ready to find the last missile."

"Well, I know I'm exhausted and won't have any trouble sleeping tonight," yawned Larry.

"Why don't we all go

do our usual routines and crawl into bed," Shara suggested.

"You're right Shara. The commander wants us to meet him at 0:800 in his office, I'll see you tomorrow," said James as he waved goodbye to his friends.

Later that night as the three friends slept, around ten an old goat named Mr. Sunny Seed was digging up a body in the sweet slumber cemetery.

Monday, January 23rd

Since Larry didn't live far from Chief Ramstein's home, he decided to walk. He looked outside, saw it was raining, and figured it would be best to wear his hooded coat. He put his coat on and started off for the chief's house. When he arrived, he knocked on the door and Mrs. Ramstein answered.

"You must be Larry." she said.

Larry nodded.

"Your two friends are already in my husband's office." She led him down the hall to the home office. "Honey, Larry is here," she called as she entered the room.

"Margaret, please don't call me 'honey' in front of the team."

Mrs. Ramstein gave a slight eye roll and went to get a class of water for Larry.

"Okay kids, do we have any new clues on where the last missile could be?" asked the chief as he folded his hands on his desk.

"No sir, we don't. But, we are planning to check the last two cemeteries just to make sure they are clean," James said.

"And after that?" asked Chief Ramstein.

"We thought we should re-check the entire city to make sure we haven't missed anything," said James.

The chief nodded in agreement and the kids took off.

Meanwhile, Angry was in the mayor's office at City Hall drinking a Koka-Kola from Burger Queen as Fire admired herself in the mirror.

Suddenly, one of Angry's gang members came running into the office. He was shaking with fear. His rat eyes were big as dinner plates and his long pink rat tail kept tapping the floor nervously.

"How dare you come bursting into my office! What do you want? And it better be important," growled Angry.

"It is, it is Angry," the rat said in his nervous rat voice. "I have some bad news. No one else would tell you but...."

"Tell me you moron!" Angry growled.

"Okay, okay, four missiles are missing," the rat blurted out before he lost what little nerve he had left.

"What!" Angry shouted as he grabbed a chair and threw it across the room; it broke into pieces when it hit the wall.

Angry stared at the rat as he said, "How? Who took them?" With his voice filled with rage, Angry stepped closer and closer to the rat.

"Now Angry, it's not my fault."

Angry paused, "Okay, tell me whose fault it is?"

"Well, it was those weird teenagers who have been running and flying all over the city. They beat up all the guys that were guarding the four missiles."   "You mean a couple of kids took my missiles?" asked Angry in a low, but dangerous voice.

            "These kids have special powers, Angry, and there are three of them."   "What do you mean 'special powers?'"

"Two of them can fly and one runs faster than our fastest Cheetah."

"I want six of my strongest guys to go to each hiding place and check on my missiles. Now!" yelled Angry.

So, six gang members took the brown van and went out in the rain to check on the missiles. It took the bad guys about an hour to check all the hiding places; they had to be careful so the super teens wouldn't see them.

They were more than a little scared to give Angry the bad news when they returned; they all knew what a terrible temper he had.

"You tell him," said Oxford the ox.

"No way, I would rather have my horns pulled out!" exclaimed Bart the bull.   "Okay, okay, we'll tell him together," said Oxford.

They went to the Mayor's office to tell Angry.

"Five of the missiles are gone, Angry, not just four." Oxford and Bart said at the same time.

"What! How can that be? "Angry said with fire coming from his eyes and his teeth gleaming. "I want to talk to all the animals that saw these so called 'superheroes'," Angry was already suspicious about how these teens got their powers. "While I talk to the animals, I want you two to go get the last missile from the storage shed and bring it here. Make sure no one sees you," Angry ordered.

Oxford and Bart and two other gangsters took the van to go get the last missile.

As the day ended the teens had not found the last missile. "I don't know where else to look, Shara said

"Me either, "said James as he sat down in the chair of Chief Ramstein's office.

"You kids have worked hard today," said the chief.

Mrs. Ramstein came into the office and said, "You

need to turn the T.V. on right away."

Chief Ramstein turned on the T.V. Instead of the regular news, everyone saw a news flash come on as the news caster said, "Important breaking news, Anger Machine Gun Muscle has taken oven the T.V. station!"

"Oh no, this can't be good," said Larry as Angry's face came on the T.V.

Angry said, "I know you snotty-nosed brats are out there somewhere. I know you took my missiles, but I still have one left. And one is enough to blow up Sunsky City. I also have figured out how you two got your powers. I know it's you Blue Necklace and Blue Watch. So you picked a couple of weak teenagers this time—well that was your mistake. I am giving you twenty-four hours to give me my missiles back and have the kids bring you to me at the mayor's office or I will blow up this city. Angry spread his arms out to show the missile sitting in the middle of the room. "No funny stuff, you have twenty four hours."

The T.V. went black.

Professor Pop had been watching T.V. in his hotel room and heard Angry's threat. This is what he had been worried about. But, he also knew it was all up to Blue Necklace and Blue Watch to save the city. He hoped they had chosen their animals wisely.
"What is he talking about, what does a blue necklace and blue watch have to do with all this?" asked the chief.

The kids knew now was the time to tell their chief about how they had gotten their powers. James turned to Mrs. Ramstein and said, "Mrs. Ramstein, would you mind making us some sandwiches? I think this is going to be a long night."

Tuesday, January 24th -
Four A.M. on planet Earth, year 3990 A.D.

In Florida, the crew of the spaceship Cornucopia was preparing for take-off for Farth, a planet in another galaxy.

The director of Food Resources was meeting with the captain of the Cornucopia. "Remember, your first order of business is to meet with the leaders of Farth. We need you to work out some kind of deal where we can buy food from them. After that is completed, tell them about the group that has been shipping food from their planet illegally. Ask them to work with us to stop the illegal transporting."

"Yes sir, I understand," said the Captain.

Two hours later the ship had been loaded and was ready to launch into space.

****

Meanwhile, back on Farth, it was nearing six and Angry's time limit was almost up.

"Alright, everybody understands the plan?" asked Chief Ramstein as he and the teen team stood around his desk.

"Yes sir," all three super heroes said.

"Okay," said the chief to his aide, "Call Angry and tell him we are ready to hand over the Blue Necklace and the Blue Watch.

Shara and James made their way to city hall and the mayor's office to give Angry what he needed.

"Their coming Angry," said Fire as she watched the duo walk up to the building on the security cameras.

"Is it the Blue Knight and Blue Princess or is it just the kids?" Angry asked.

"Just the two dumb kids carrying the watch and necklace in their hands," said Fire.

"Excellent! Unlock the doors," Angry told two guards as he smiled with evil glee.

Shara and James walked up to the building and waited for the doors to open.

"I hate giving these pieces of jewelry to Angry," Shara sighed.

"We don't have a choice," James said as the doors opened and he and Shara walked in.

"Follow me you two," said a gang member who led Shara and James to the elevator.

The elevator opened to the mayor's office and Angry stood there with one hand on the missile and used the other hand to motion James and Shara into the office.

"Welcome, I am glad to see that you have come to your senses," laughed Angry as he stepped in front of the missile, leaving it unguarded by the large window.

"Oh my gosh!" exclaimed Fire when she walked into the office and saw Shara. "Is that what you look like without your friend the necklace? Oh you poor, ugly, fat thing!" she laughed.

"But now you," Fire said as she walked over to touch James' shoulder. "You are as handsome as before you put on the watch."

"Enough Fire!" growled Angry.

"Oh, alright," Fire sighed as she ran a finger down James' cheek. "I will see you later," she purred.

"Let's get down to business. I want that necklace and watch. I want the power to rule the whole Morld," said Angry as he grabbed a jewelry box from the desk and walked over to James and Shara. "Okay, put those two beautiful pieces right in here," he passed the box to James.

James put the watch in, giving Angry a dirty look, but said nothing.

Shara took the box from James and gently laid the necklace into it and said, "You won't get away with this Angry."

"Oh, but my dear, I already have," Angry said and took the box from Shara's hands.

Suddenly the window behind Angry shattered and Larry flew into the room. Before Angry could say or do anything, Larry had the missile and was flying out the opposite window.

"I guess this isn't your day, Angry," James said as he turned into the Blue Knight.

"No! No way." yelled Angry. He took off out the window after Larry.

"Fire looked at Shara and gasped, "That's impossible, Angry has the Blue Watch." Then it dawned on her, "That means you are still...."

"Yes, I am," smiled Shara, as she turned into the Blue Princess. "Oh, and by the way, James thinks you are ugly."

As Fire and Shara did battle in the mayor's office, Angry's gang members ran as far away from the city as they could. They hadn't counted on the police surrounding the city. A few gang members and robbers tried to fight the police but failed, the rest gave up and were arrested.

"I never thought you were all that pretty Blue Princess," said Fire to Shara as she shot a stream of fire at her.

"Good thing I don't care much for what you think," Shara said as she put out the fire with a blast of water.

The blast was so hard it knocked Fire down, and then Shara made her move. She squirted more water into

Fire's face.

Fire screamed, "My makeup," and reached both hands to her face.

It was then that Shara grabbed the Red Necklace and ripped it from Fire's neck.

As Shara stared, Fire turned back into Felisha, the normal cat that looked just as she always had.

Shara quickly backed away from Felisha so that she could not grab the necklace back. The police came in to the office and arrested the now crying Felisha.

"I am going to see if James needs any help," Shara told the police.

"Oh, and by the way Felisha, your mascara is smeared," Shara smiled and took off.

Angry had followed Larry to the Majestic Mountains with James not far behind.

Larry landed on the Mountain and was exhausted from carrying the missile and flying so far. He turned to see Angry land not far from him.

"You seem to be out of breath my friend," said Angry. "I believe you have something that belongs to me—six something's to be exact, and I want them back... now."

Larry tried to catch his breath as he said, "You gotta get through me first."

Angry walked closer to Larry, "Ha, you are almost ready to pass out as it is. You aren't going to be a problem for me."

"But, I might," said James as he landed between Larry and Angry.

"Is being the Blue Knight the best you've got? Because this," Angry moved his hands down his body, "is not the best I've got."

James watched as Angry turned into the Black Knight. Angry's body armor was shiny black with large spikes sticking out all over. His helmet covered his entire head, except for two openings for his eyes and two for the two horns on top of his head. The Black Knight held a large mace in one hand and a big round shield with spikes all around it in the other.

"Bring it on, Blue Boy," The Black Knight said as he motioned with his two fingers for James to come to him.

"You think you are the only one to keep a secret?" James said as he held out a hand and a blue shield formed. "Think again."

"Just adding a scrawny blue shield isn't going to help you Blue Boy."

"Enough talking, let's find out," James said in a deep, quite voice.

The two animals charged each other and the duel began.

After about twenty minutes of fighting, James was getting very tired. The Black Knight is just too strong for me, he thought.

Shara arrived just as the Black Knight hit James with the mace and James crumpled to the ground.

"James!" Shara screamed, worried her friend might be hurt. She started to go toward him.

The Black Knight turned to face Shara, "Good, you are here too, now I won't have to go far to kill you, like I just killed your blue friend," He gave her an evil smile as he walked away from James and toward her.

The Black Knight thought James was dead, but truth was, James was watching through narrowed eyes as Angry moved toward Shara. His heart tightened with fear for Shara for he couldn't let anything happen to her. She was so beautiful with or without the blue necklace.

Shara stood facing the Black Knight. Blue Necklace had given Shara a light, but very strong body suit armor of blue, especially for this battle.

"Nice suit," said the Black Knight said as he charged toward Shara.

The Black Knight barely saw the blue streak as it went by him. There standing beside Shara was James, his brown eyes flashing.

The Black Knight growled, "I can take both of you on," and he began to grow larger and larger.

"Let's show this rabbit he isn't the only one who can grow around her," James said and he grew larger.

"You are so right James," Shara said as she too grew.

Now the three giants faced off for battle. The two superheroes fought the Black Knight with everything they had, but in the end the two heroes lay defeated at the Black Knight's feet, he held his mace above James.

James looked up and said, "Do you believe in a being greater than yourself?"

"No, I only believe in me, and now I will rule everything." The Black Knight prepared to bring the mace down on James' head.

"Well, you might want to change your mind about that." said James.

Suddenly, a bright white sword appeared and blocked the mace from hitting James. Both Shara and James looked up and followed the weapon to the hand that held it. Standing there was a beautiful white dolphin wearing glowing white armor.

"It's the Dolphin God!" whispered Shara.

"Yes!" agreed James.

The mighty Dolphin God looked at the Black Knight and said, "Black Watch, you have used your powers unwisely. Change your ways or do battle with me."

"I am not afraid of you. I not only have the powers the scientists gave this body, but I have my powers as well. I am greater than you white dolphin. Let's do battle."

"So be it," the Dolphin God said as he used his powers to move Larry, Shara and James to a safe place. Then the Dolphin God pulled another white sword from his side. Saying nothing, he lifted the swords above his head and the ground under the Black Knight began to shake.

The Black Knight looked around in terror, but before he could even scream, the ground opened up and began to drag him down. Suddenly, the Black Knight seemed to explode into a thousand pieces.

From the smoke rose a giant Black Dragon. The kids watched as the Dragon flew out of the hole and landed by the White Knight.

"Now dolphin, you and I will finally battle each other," said the Dragon. He roared and a great billow of fire and smoke shot out of his mouth toward the White Knight.

The Dolphin God made a cross from his two white swords and held it out in front of him. When the dragon's fire hit the sword it bounced back hitting the dragon, causing him to fall back into the hole. The White Knight touched one sword to the ground and the hole closed up forever. The kids stared wide eyed at the Dolphin God. Even Larry seemed in awe. Without another word, the Dolphin God vanished.

Wednesday, January 25th

As Wednesday dawned clear and bright, the FBI had already begun removing the six missiles from the mountain and returning to Duke Air Force Base.

"Hey Captain," called one of the FBI agents, "Can you come here a minute?"

"What is it agent Morris?"

"Look," Morris pointed to a severed arm laying on a rock.

"It's Angry's arm. Let's bag it and take it to our secure lab. At least the Black Watch was on the arm that was destroyed," said the Captain.

"Yes, sir," said agent Morris.

Back in Sunsky City, the citizens were busy cleaning up as the police continued to bring in bad guys. Shara, James, and Larry also helped to clean up the mess in their city.

"Wow, it's a lot slower cleaning up without our superpowers," said Shara

"It sure is. I wonder what the mayor will decide about us keeping the Blue Watch and Blue Necklace?" wondered James.

"And don't forget my suit," said Larry.

"The military will be the one to decide that," said Shara.

"Well, at least Professor Pop has his Blue and Red Necklaces back as well as the Blue Watch and he doesn't have to worry about the Black Watch; it was totally destroyed. So, I guess it is up to the Professor what happens to them," said James.

"Yeah," said Shara, a little sadness in her voice. Would James still like her now that she was no longer skinny and beautiful?

James looked at Shara and he knew what she was thinking, so he took her paw and said, "I think you are more beautiful than ever Shara. I'd like to take you on a date when this mess is all cleaned up."

Shara's eyes sparkled, she smiled and nodded yes.

"Okay, okay enough you two," laughed Larry. "Let's get back to work."

The rest of the day the teens worked hard to clean their city up.

Thursday, January 26th

As Shara came down for breakfast at seven her mom said, "Shara, honey, I've invited Larry and James over. I've made lots of snacks and I thought you three would like to just hang out, relax, and watch movies. They should be here around ten. I checked with their parents and it's okay for them to miss school today."

"Thanks mom, that sounds great, and I'll have to time to get ready before they get here." She especially wanted to look nice for James.

The phone rang as Shara sat down to a healthy breakfast of oatmeal, orange juice, and toast.

Her mom answered the phone and said to Shara," It's See Nosey."

Shara got up and went to the phone. "Hey See, how's it going?"

"Just waiting on the bus and thought I would call you for a quick chat, and to say I am so proud of what you did, congrats girlfriend, you are awesome!"

"Thanks, See," Shara said as she blushed. "How is Andrew?"

"He is great and he got a new haircut. It's a green Mohawk—he looks so cute."

Shara smiled and said, "I bet he does. By the way, how come you liked Andrew while he was still in the gang?"

"Because we have been neighbors and friends since we were ten and I knew he was good at heart, he was just a little confused. Speaking of my sweetie, he is waiting out front to walk with me to the bus stop so I gotta go. Talk to you later."

"Yeah, have a good day and tell Andrew I said 'hi',"

Shara hung up the phone.

The rest of the day, Shara, James, and Larry watched movies, played video games, and munched on all their favorite snack foods.

It was four o'clock in Professor Pop's lab and he was thinking about how well James and Shara had done having super powers. After all, the necklace and watch had chosen them.

At the same time, the mayor was also thinking about how nice it would be to have the Blue Knight and Blue Princess around any time he needed them to fight crime. The citizens of Sunsky City would be very happy too. Even though the A and B gangs were gone and the Cruddy-Fair neighborhood cleaned up, new gangs as well as others could start up in their city or across the country.

The mayor picked up the phone to call Professor Pop. He wanted to ask the scientist if the kids could keep the necklace and watch.

"Hello Professor, it's the mayor and I have something to ask you," said the mayor when Pop answered the phone.

"I think I already know what you are going to ask. Can the kids keep the watch and necklace?"

"Yes, that is what I was going to ask you," said the mayor

"Well, the necklace and the watch did choose them, and I think the Morld could use a couple super heroes," said the Pop.

They agreed that Professor Pop would bring the Blue Necklace and the Blue Watch to the Mayor's office the next day.

James, Shara, and Larry all went to bed that night thinking about what it was like to have super powers and how much they would miss having them.

Friday, January 27th

The mayor made three early morning phone calls and told the kids' parents to not let them watch T.V. or talk to any of their friends. He had a great surprise for them. He told the parents to have the kids at Central Park at noon. The parents all agreed, though the mayor did not tell them what was going to happen. The mayor spent the morning getting the park decorated for the big announcement. Balloons and streamers filled the air and posters were hung everywhere.

At eleven-thirty a long black limousine pulled up in front of Larry's house. The driver came up to the door and knocked. When Larry's mom answered, he said," Madam, if you, your husband, and Master Larry would please come with me."

When Larry stepped into the limo he saw James, Shara, and their families already sitting in the large car.

"What's going on?" Shara asked.

"Not a clue," said James.

Soon the limo pulled up to a large stage in Central Park. When the kids got out they were greeted by a large crowd cheering at the top of their lungs. They saw posters, balloons, and streamers.

"It must be like a 'Thank-you' celebration," said Larry as the three kids climbed the steps to the stage.

There they saw the Mayor, Professor Pop, Chief Ramstein and many of their friends as well as thousands of animals they didn't know.

The crowd went wild as the three teens walked up to stand by the mayor. The mayor raised his hands to quiet the crowd.

"As everyone knows, these are three very special

young people standing next to me today," said the mayor

Again the crowd erupted with cheers. After they quieted down the mayor continued.

"On behalf of your government, and all the animals of Morld, we have a great favor to ask of you three. Would you consider continuing your service as super heroes?" asked the mayor.

The crowd became totally quiet as everyone waited for the teens to answer.

James, Larry, and Shara looked at each other; they knew that they wanted this more than anything in the Morld. They each said yes.

With that, the crowd cheered. Professor Pop was the first to come up to the teens. He presented James with the Blue Watch and Shara with the Blue Necklace. The teens put on the magical items and instantly the Blue Knight and the Blue Princess appeared.

Then Chief Ramstein walked up to Larry and handed him the suit. Larry held the suit high above his head and everyone cheered for their super heroes.

After several minutes the crowd again grew quiet. The mayor came up to James with a piece of paper in his hand and said, "We have all discussed this James and we want you to be the leader of the teen team."

James looked at Larry and Shara, they each nodded their agreement.

"I would be honored," said James as he took the official paper from the mayor.

The mayor turned to the crowd and lifted his hand towards the teens, "I give you our protectors," he said with pride.

The crowd cheered and cheered and was ready to celebrate.

The rest of the day and most of the night parties were going on all over the Morld.

Saturday, January 28th

       Saturday the parties continued all day and again into the night.

       At the same time in a prison for female animals, Felisha was starting her eight year sentence. The judge had cut her sentence from sixteen years to eight because he felt that Felisha had been possessed by the Red Necklace and therefore what had happened had not been entirely her fault. Still, the eight years was to be spent doing hard labor. As well as prison time, Felisha's nursing degree was declared invalid and she would never again work as a nurse. Felisha watched all the celebrations on the T.V. in prison and knew she had made the wrong choice.

       At a party at the mayor's house, James put his arm around Shara and said, "You are beautiful on the inside, Shara, and that is what is important."
Shara smiled up at James and said, "Yes, I know that now."

THE END

ABOUT THE AUTHOR

Michael Stone is twenty-five years old and lives in Paulden, Arizona with his family and two schnauzers. He works at YEI in Prescott, Arizona. Michael has always loved to tell stories, even as a young boy he would make up imitative tales. Michael lives with autism, this affects his speech to a small degree, but it affects his ability to write to a greater degree. Because Michael cannot physically write his stories he simply dictates them to a willing typist (usually his mom or Anita). Michael has proven that a disability does not have to stop a person from realizing their dreams, so dream on and never stop.

www.ingramcontent.com/pod-product-compliance
Lightning Source LLC
Chambersburg PA
CBHW070445170726
48291CB00005B/1609